I0736442

RAPUNZEL UNTAMED

USA TODAY BESTSELLING AUTHOR

ERIN BEDFORD

Rapunzel Untamed © 2019-2020
Embrace the Fantasy Publishing, LLC

All rights reserved under the International and Pan-American Copyright Conventions. No part of this book may be reproduced or transmitted in any form or by any means, electronic or mechanical, including photocopying, recording, or by any information storage and retrieval system, without permission in writing from the publisher.

This is a work of fiction. Names, places, characters and incidents are either the product of the author's imagination or are used fictitiously, and any resemblance to any actual persons, living or dead, organizations, events or locales is entirely coincidental.

Warning: the unauthorized reproduction or distribution of this copyrighted work is illegal. Criminal copyright infringement, including infringement without monetary gain, is investigated by the FBI and is punishable by up to 5 years in prison and a fine of $250,000.

Edited by: Elemental Editing and Proofreading

Cover Design by: Moonstruck Cover Design and Photography

Also by Erin Bedford

The Underground Series
Chasing Rabbits
Chasing Cats
Chasing Princes
Chasing Shadows
Chasing Hearts
The Crimes of Alice
Hatter's Heart
Cheshire's Smile

The Mary Wiles Chronicles
Marked by Hell
Bound by Hell
Deceived by Hell
Tempted by Hell

Starcrossed Dragons
Riding Lightning
Grinding Frost
Swallowing Fire
Pounding Earth

The Crimson Fold
Until Midnight
Until Dawn
Until Sunset

Curse of the Fairy Tales
Rapunzel Untamed
Rapunzel Unveiled

Rapunzel Unchained

Her Angels
Heaven's Embrace
Heaven's A Beach
Heaven's Most Wanted

House of Durand
Indebted to the Vampires
Wanted by the Vampires
Protected by the Vampires
Embrace of the Vampires
Tempted by the Butler
Loved by the Vampires
Huntress of the Vampires

Academy of Witches
Witching On A Star
As You Witch
Witch You Were Here
Just Witch It
Summer Witchin'

Children of the Fallen
Death In Her Eyes
Fire In Her Blood

The Beast of the Fae Court
Granting Her Wish
Vampire CEO

RAPUNZEL UNTAMED

USA TODAY BESTSELLING AUTHOR

ERIN BEDFORD

Chapter 1

There was a bird in my tower. A little white bird with black speckles. It chirped and walked around the gray stone floor in front of me as if it hadn't just entered my home.

It really didn't bother me. I was happy for the company after, well, I didn't really know how long I'd been here, but either way, it was nice to see something that wasn't my own feet or the gray wall across from me.

For a long time, all I knew was silence. Even the sound of my voice had disappeared. Though, that may have been because I'd stopped speaking. Eventually, even your own company gets tiresome.

As I watched the bird with growing curiosity, my mind still muddled from the loneliness, I wondered if I was hallucinating. It wouldn't be the first time. When you had only yourself for company, sometimes your mind did what it could to save your sanity.

I spent a whole month—or maybe it was only an hour, I didn't know—once thinking I was having a tea party with a short old man and his crazy rabbit. A door mouse kept stealing my cup and making up such nonsense that I began to believe they were the ones who were mad. It took me a while to figure out that it was my own mind playing with me.

Stupid idiot.

If I couldn't tell that was a hallucination, I surely didn't trust myself enough not to be fooled by this one as well. But why a bird? Surely, if I was going to hallucinate anything, it would be getting out of here. Or maybe even a big blueberry pie. It was my favorite. Or at least, I thought it was. I hardly remembered my own face, let alone what I liked or disliked.

Back to the bird. Its incessant chirping was beginning to annoy me, which could only mean the likelihood of it being real had gone considerably up.

At first, I tried to talk to the bird, but my mouth wouldn't work from disuse, my tongue too fat for my mouth. It didn't help that the fog in my head was thick enough to cut with a knife.

I giggled to myself, the sound foreign to me as it bounced off the walls. The sound spooked my newfound friend, who flapped its wings and flew back out the single window in my stone prison.

Outside, there was light. How had I not noticed this? For a long time, I'd only ever seen a dullness, like I was stuck between night and day. I spent a lot of time staring at that window.

It was big enough for a person to get through and it taunted me endlessly. It would tell me, "Here's your freedom. Come and get it."

Even though my prison stood thousands of feet above the ground, sadly that much they let me remember. If I hadn't been chained to the wall, I'd have happily jumped. Death had to be better than this endless nothingness. At least, that was what I told myself.

Today, however, I was happy I never took that plunge. I would have missed this change. A change I wasn't quite sure was a good thing. Of course, anything was better than what I had, so I decided to look at the tower half full.

I giggled again. "Tower half full," I muttered to myself, saliva falling out of my mouth as I tried to form the words.

A loud horn blared and I jerked in place. I didn't get far, the chains bound to my arms and legs giving me barely a foot of movement where I sat on the floor.

My head swiveled to the window, and I tried to stretch myself toward it, angling my head to see out, but I was too far away. All I could see was the endless blue sky. The sounds, though, were different. I couldn't remember what I should be hearing, but it wasn't silence, which made it a positive in my book.

What I found most alarming was the amount of sound that began to accumulate. At first, it had been just the birds chirping, then the horns blaring, but now there was a distinct amount of voices as if a crowd had begun to gather.

This must be another trick. Some kind of illusion to torture me more. Why else would I suddenly start seeing and hearing things? Unless I'd really lost it this time.

I'd long since forgotten why I was in this tower to begin with. Counting the days had ended when I lost the will to care. I had hoped eventually I would just die, but they had made sure that would never happen. Whoever they were. That had been forgotten as well. I didn't even remember what it felt like to be hungry or tired. Even needing to use the bathroom would have been something different. Though, thinking about it, sitting in my own filth would not have been pleasant.

A voice clear as day above the roar of the others jerked my attention back to the window. "I'm telling you, I'll be fine."

Someone was coming. For me to hear them, they must be close. Panic didn't well up inside of me, there would be no point. I was helpless to whoever breached my tower walls. I couldn't pray because I'd long learned the deities weren't going to save me. If they were, they'd have done it a long time ago.

I waited with bated breath. Half of me hoped for my salvation and the other half for my destruction. Would today finally be the day they put me out of my misery? Had I paid enough for my crimes to be let go?

My heart, which I had almost forgot could beat, raced as a dreaded excitement filled me. I hadn't felt anything other than numbness for, well, forever. The foreign feeling in my chest as I watched the hand find a good grip ratcheted up and up until I feared my heart would jump out of my chest.

A hand curled around the stone at the bottom of the window. My head angled to the side. My eyes zeroed in on the intruder. Another hand took up residence next to the first, and then a spiky, ash blond head of hair peeked up from beneath. A full face followed it, and then a body, a clearly male form, which dragged himself over the lip of the window to land on the ground at my feet.

"Man, what a climb," the man panted, his eyes tightly shut.

I took that moment to scan the individual. An angular face sat beneath the head of spiked up hair, his nose was straight and not at all crooked. A thin set of lips graced his face above a strong jaw, which sat on top of narrow shoulders. His clothing was like nothing I'd ever seen before.

A forest green jacket with bronze colored buttons and strange medallions decorating the shoulders fell open on the floor beside him. A black shirt stretched across his muscles, allowing me to see the defined ridges of his stomach. The shirt was tucked into a pair of pants the same color as the jacket. The pants hugged his hips, the sides of the legs poofing out at the knee before they ended in a pair of shiny black boots.

Honestly, I didn't remember much of anything when it came to clothing. For all I knew, what he wore was perfectly normal. I'd only ever seen the flimsy white gown I'd been put in. Or put on. I wasn't sure how I ended up in it. Just that it was there. Strange or not, I'd have been happy to wear what he wore instead.

However, I couldn't imagine the man before me would be interested in switching outfits. The image of him wearing my gown made me giggle.

One mahogany brown eye popped open to stare at me. I didn't bother to pretend like I wasn't watching him. He was my delusion after all. I could stare if I wanted to.

"Adam!" a voice called out, annoyance lacing the word. Was that his name? Adam?

This Adam character scrambled to his hands and knees, his eyes scanning over me. If I could feel much of anything, I'd have said my body flushed, but alas, all I felt was numbness. What I would kill for even a stomachache.

The voice called his name again, and he turned his head slightly to the side, "I'm here. Come on up, the view is great," he said this with a cheeky grin on his lips as he shuffled toward me.

Reaching out a hand, he cupped the side of my face, turning it more toward him. "And who might you be, sweetheart?" When I didn't answer, his eyes and hand went to my long, pale hair. "Or maybe I should just call you Rapunzel?"

Something clicked in my mind at the name, something that made me laugh. It must have been a scary laugh, because Adam jumped away from me to stand near the window once more. Giving me a curious look, he then turned and poked his head out of the tower.

"Hurry up, would you? There's something up here you've just got to see." Adam leaned back from the window, that humorous grin still on his lips.

"So, sweetheart," Adam began again, his hands tucked into the pockets of his pants. They looked even better on him from this angle. A strange tingling buzzed inside of me, the first hint of any sort of feeling. It was so sudden it made me gasp.

The small sound caused Adam to frown. He stared at me with a mixture of curiosity and suspicion, as if I were the one who had broken into his tower. Really, he should be so lucky.

A grunt followed by a curse was my only warning before another body came tumbling onto the floor. This time, though, the intruder didn't fall at my feet but rather on them.

Chapter 2

The sudden contact caused me to squeak in surprise, and I jerked my legs back as far as I was able, which still didn't remove the person from them. Soft, white hair fell against my ankles in a tumbled mess over half of the man's face. It had to be my lucky day. Two men, more men than I'd seen—well, ever—and they were both here at the same time. If this was a delusion, and I still wasn't ruling it out, then it was one hell of a way to torture me.

The white-haired man groaned and rubbed the back of his head, sitting up off my legs. He didn't seem to have noticed me despite my less than brave squeaking. Leaning forward over one knee, one gloved hand rubbed his forehead. Unlike Adam, this one's face had soft curves and kissable lips, his nose just the right size for his face.

His clothes were just as unusual as Adam's. A long, white cloak lined with gold and red embellishments covered most of his body, but the neck of it opened to show a bare muscled chest. Markings I didn't recognize decorated the skin of his chest and stomach before disappearing into his white pants. He, too, wore shiny black boots, except his weren't trying to eat his pants like Adam's.

When his eyes opened—a shocking golden color—he didn't even look at me, but to where Adam stood. "Why didn't you warn me of the lip?"

Adam grinned, exchanging a look with me before saying, "You should look before you leap, Luke."

The golden eyed man named Luke, chuckled and rubbed the back of his head sheepishly. "What can I say? I'm a daredevil. But Zane's going to kill you, you know. For coming up here by yourself."

Lifting a shoulder, Adam moved away from the wall and toward me. "I'm not worried about him. I'm worried about her." He pointed a long finger in my direction, causing Luke to finally notice me.

Those golden eyes landed on me, widening in the corners as Luke took in my form. When his gaze fell on my legs where one of

10

his hands still rested, he jolted back, a nervous chuckle releasing. "Sorry about that. I didn't see you there."

I didn't say anything. There was nothing to say. I didn't know these men, aside from their names, I also didn't know what they wanted with me. Were they here to save me or kill me? Both prospects caused hope to swell in me.

As another body came crawling into my tower, which was becoming smaller by the minute, I squashed my hope back down where it belonged. This one had short hair the color of dried blood. Why I knew what dried blood even looked like, I didn't want to terry on. Some things were better forgotten.

Unlike the other two, he didn't fall into the tower, but stepped in with a calm aloofness. Hazel eyes hidden behind a pair of glasses on a stern face swept the room. They first landed on Adam and Luke, making them soften slightly, before they landed on me.

If looks could kill, I'd have been dead on the spot.

"What's this?" the man asked, caution in his voice. The blackness of his shirt and pants tailored to fit him. The material pulled across his chest ever so slightly as he moved toward me. On closer inspection, his hair wasn't short but tied back in a long braid that swung behind him, along with the cross hanging from his neck and dangling above his navel.

I didn't move, let alone breathe as he knelt before me. His eyes searched my face, and then he dipped his head down to my neck. I tensed as he inhaled deeply.

Pulling away from me, he glanced back at Luke and Adam. "She's human. Or at least appears to be." Turning his eyes back to me, his hands took hold of one of the metal cuffs around my wrist. "There seems to be some kind of enchantment on these."

I flinched at the contact of his cold hand on my skin. I hadn't been touched in... I didn't know how long, but it was a long time to go without contact, without comfort. If just this little bit of feeling affected me this much, I didn't know what I would do if someone was to hug me. I promised myself right then that I would not moan like some cat in heat. No siree.

"An enchantment?" Adam asked, moving closer as well. "Can you remove it?" Adam smiled down at me. "This is Zane. He's a master spell caster. If anyone can break your bonds, it's him."

Brow furrowed, I nodded, though I only understood half of what he was saying. I kept an eye on the three men in the room and one on the window where the sound of someone climbing hadn't stopped. It made my head hurt and my eyes ache to divide my attention. Finally, deciding that anyone coming in couldn't be that bad if the others in my tower were anything to go by, I turned my full attention on the man with glasses. Someone so pretty couldn't be here to kill me, right?

Pushing his glasses up his nose with one finger, Zane studied my binds with such intensity that I wondered if he saw them at all. "There are sigils here that I haven't seen before, but it seems like some kind of stasis spell."

I tried to angle my head back to see what he was talking about, but all I could see was the grey metal of my cuffs. If there were sigils—whatever those were—I couldn't see them.

"Stasis?" Luke asked this time, his head tilting to the side adorably. "Like suspended animation?"

Nodding, Zane leaned back from the cuffs and stared down at me. "Whoever put her here wanted her to live for a very long time."

I stared back at him defiantly. I already figured out that little bit, however, if they were going to question what I knew about the lot of it then they were shit out of luck.

"Then we shouldn't release her." A deep, husky voice announced the new person's arrival. My eyes jerked from Zane's hypnotic stare to the window where a new figure stood.

For a second, I thought I saw double, but then I realized the man must be Luke's twin. They were the same in almost every way except for where Luke had a cheery disposition, this one had a scowl on his face. Black as ink hair, in the same kind of shaggy style as Luke, sat on his head, one side of it styled to cover one eye. The other had the same brilliant gold that had entranced me before.

As well as looking similar, their clothing was identical except the color. Where Luke wore light colors, this one wore black, the gold and red embellishments the same as well.

Hmmm. Interesting. Who were these men? If someone had sent them to finish me off, they hadn't done a very good job picking someone to frighten me. The only emotion that was waking up beneath the numbness was attraction and curiosity. Though, I wasn't sure which was the stronger one.

"Blake." Adam sighed and shook his head. That ash blond hair moving with the movement before turning his eyes back to me. "We can't just leave her here."

"Why the hell not?" Blake growled, crossing his arms over his chest as he glared at me. "As you said, she's in stasis. It's not like she's going to die, and we don't need any more problems so close to our trials. Not to mention the election." He gave Adam a pointed look. I didn't understand most of what he was talking about, but if they left me here, I surely would go mad...well madder.

"We can't leave her," Zane argued, shifting to face Blake. "If we don't take her someone else will and they might not be so kind. Could you really leave someone so helpless to their fate?"

Blake's lips twisted down as he debated whether he could leave me.

His brother grabbed his arm and grinned.

"Just think of the stories. We'd be like knights rescuing the damsel in distress." Luke fisted the air with a grin. "She's like that princess in the story."

"Rapunzel," Adam supplied for him, his eyes twinkling down on me. "Just look at all that hair." He gestured down to the mass of silky blonde strands curled around the floor beneath my feet and most of theirs.

There was that name again. It wasn't mine. I was sure of it, but it was familiar in some way. More familiar than anything else I'd seen today. A voice in my head started to chant, and it came pouring out of my mouth.

"Rapunzel. Rapunzel. Let down your hair," I cackled maniacally, causing four pairs of eyes to lock on me and one grumpy twin to scoff.

"She's crazy," the newest, muscled delusion said, throwing his hand in my direction. He wasn't wrong.

Adam's grin deepened, a dimple I wanted to lick appearing on his cheek. "Maybe so, but how can you resist a damsel in distress? Especially, one that looks like that!"

What could I say? A few years—at least—and I still had my good looks. Or at least they thought they were good. I could look like a frog for all I knew. Warts and all. Too bad my mind wasn't in as good of shape.

"I know this may be difficult for you," the dark twin sneered, his arms crossed over his impressive chest. "But think with your head instead of your dick. If she's locked up, it's probably for a good reason." He gestured toward me, the sneer on his face deepening. "She could be a drainer. Have you ever thought of that?"

"Blake," Zane said near my head, "don't be unkind. I smelled her myself. She's human."

"All the more reason to leave her here," Blake cried out, his nose wrinkling in disgust. Clearly, humans didn't rate very high on his meter.

"Dude." Luke shook his head sadly. "Don't be such an asshole. She needs our help. The least we can do is give it to her."

"I'm not being an asshole, Lucas," he snapped, stepping closer to his twin. "I'm being practical. Something we need to be at a time like this."

Adam let out an audible sigh, rubbing his forehead. "We'll take her to the hospital, and then the council can figure out what to do with her next," Adam continued where Luke left off, my head jerking back and forth between the three of them. "Alright?" His brown eyes moved around the room.

"Absolutely." Luke raised his hand in the air.

He stared down Blake when he didn't answer until he finally muttered, "Fine."

"Zane?" They all looked at the man still working on my metal binds. "What do you say?"

"Agreed. Now, let's see if we can get you out of these." Zane offered me a smile, the first I'd seen on him since he arrived. I'd have thought he hated me as much as Blake, but the softness there told me differently.

Staring curiously up at him, I then realized he wanted a response. "Okay," I croaked out, my voice still not entirely up to par.

Zane muttered a few words I didn't understand, which resulted in the cuffs warming against my skin before they fell to the ground with a loud clank. Lowering my arms, I rubbed where the metal had sat, a weird tingling sensation spreading through my body. I dragged my legs up to fold underneath me, aware of the four sets of eyes watching me closely.

"So..." Luke drew out, his eyes blinking widely. "How do you feel?"

At his question, I assessed my body. I felt stiff and strange like I'd been asleep for far too long. Which I supposed made sense based on how long I'd been there. The biggest thing that stood out was how much I itched.

My hand reached up and rubbed my nose, soothing feeling there before descending onto my arms and sides.

"What is she doing?" Blake growled, irritation clear in his voice.

"I believe she is scratching an itch," Zane answered with a laugh. The others—aside from Blake—chuckled as well. The sound sent goosebumps on my already itchy skin.

When I was done scratching, I turned back to them. My eyes darted to the window and without warning, I scrambled across the floor. The men jumped out of my way before hands grabbed for me.

"She's going for the window. Stop her!" Blake shouted before jumping in front of me.

A warm hand landed on my arm and dragged me away from the window. I kicked and scratched at the hand, which ended up being Adam's, as I tried to get to the opening.

"Let me go," I yelled, suddenly panicking at being caged back up. I needed to see outside, and that window was the only way in or out of the tower.

"We can't let you kill yourself," Adam argued back, struggling to hold on to me.

Suddenly, something strange and cold hit my body. I couldn't move. Why couldn't I move?

"Seriously?" Blake complained. "You're a mage. Use magic. I can't believe you're supposed to be the next Arch Mage."

Adam stopped trying to hold me when he realized I wasn't going to move. Not for the lack of trying, because I was really trying. With a frown and a scratch of his head, Adam said, "You shouldn't use magic on someone who's been under a spell for such a long period of time. You never know how the magic will react with one another."

My eyes, which were stuck on Adam, couldn't see Blake, but I hoped he was rightly guilty. At least, he sounded forlorn when he answered back, "Oh. Well, at least now she's not fighting."

"But she also can't tell us what she was doing either," Zane announced and then suddenly I could move again. Collapsing onto the ground, I wiggled my jaw and shoved my hair from my face as I glared at Blake.

Adam knelt beside me. "Sorry about Blake. He can be a little impatient. Why were you going for the window?"

I flipped my hair the other way so I could look at him. "I want to see."

"See?" Adam's brows furrowed and then Zane came up beside him.

"Isn't it obvious? She's been trapped here staring at that window. She doesn't want to jump. She wants to look out of it."

There was a chorus of o's through the tower that made me want to roll my eyes. When they were done realizing I didn't have a death wish—which I wasn't saying I didn't have—Zane helped me to my feet. "Go ahead. It's alright. We'll wait here."

Hesitating, fearful they would stop me again, I slowly crawled across the floor and made my way to the window ledge.

I wasn't sure what I expected to see, but no way in my wildest hallucinations would I have thought up this, and I'd had some crazy ones. Metal and glass buildings as tall as the sky reached up to touch the clouds and stretched on as far as the eye could see.

Below the tower was what was supposed to be a forest of trees and green, but it was overloaded with broken stone, and off to the side was a fountain that no longer ran. At one point, the area probably was the height of a city, but now it was nothing more than a mess of ruins.

Except for my tower sticking out of the middle of it.

Glancing down, people congregated around the bottom. There was a mixture of sounds filling my ears. The people, my friends the birds, and a low buzzing. The last one I couldn't discern where it was coming from. Not until it was staring me in the face.

I jerked back as a metal eyeball flew up to the window. It blinked its metal eyelid at me, its pupil zeroing in on me. I reached out to touch it, mesmerized by the contraption, but a hand grabbed my shoulder and pulled me back in.

"Get lost." Blake shot a little bolt of light out of his finger, making the floating eyeball spin in a circle before going in a random direction.

"Don't touch that," Blake snapped at me, before he realized he was still touching me and released me like I had a disease. Giving him a curious look, I turned from the window and to the men in my tower.

"So, what now?" I stood from the ground and stretched my arms up in the air. I tried not to notice the way their eyes followed my movements or how they lingered on my chest. My breasts apparently didn't have the same idea as me because the tips peaked at the attention or maybe it was the sudden burst of cold against my skin.

"Where did that door come from?" Blake asked, pointing a finger behind Luke.

"It must have been cloaked until I released the cuffs," Zane explained, moving over to examine it.

Made of a deep brown wood, the door in question hadn't been there before. I'd have remembered, I was sure of it. As we stared at it, the door flew open, banging against the wall, and sending gusts of cool air through the room. Well, if that wasn't an invitation to get out, I didn't know what was.

I shivered slightly, wrapping my arms around myself. New clothes were the first thing on my list of things to do...right after I stuff myself silly and take a shower.

"Here." Adam took his jacket off and draped it over my shoulders.

Slipping my arms into it, I smiled appreciatively up at him. "Thank you." It hung past my fingertips and warmed against my skin. I breathed in the material, sighing at the masculine scent mixed into the fabric.

"Your voice is getting better." Luke came around and studied me. He reached out to touch me, and I jerked away. He dropped his hands, a blush on his cheeks. "Sorry, the medic in me doesn't really have boundaries. Is it okay if I check your throat?"

Frowning at him, I nodded.

"I'm not going to hurt you," he explained, as his fingers prodded my neck. "I'm just checking for any kind of swelling or bruising." The wind caused his pale hair to fall across his face. He shoved it back over his ear and his brows furrowed, his attention fully on me.

"Well? Is she fine or not?" Blake snapped, impatiently tapping his foot. That single golden eye pretended to look bored, but the way it kept locking onto me showed that the dark twin was more than a bit curious.

23

I fluttered my eyelashes in his direction, making him scowl and turn away.

"You're alright. I'm sure your voice is just rusty from disuse." Dropping his hands, Luke smiled at me, his eyes the same level as mine. It was hard to tell before since I'd been on the floor, but he and I were about the same height. Blake as well, though I doubted he'd stand next to me even if I asked. Zane and Adam were both more than a foot taller than me, but since they were wearing boots and I was barefoot, it might be a bit less than that.

"Well, shall we get you out of here?" Adam offered me his arm, his dimple flashing once more.

I hesitated at first. I didn't know these men. I had no idea of knowing if they were going to hurt me or kill me. For all I knew, they were going to sell me off as a sex slave. I did know that they could get me out of here, and I wanted that more than anything in the world.

Pushing down the doubt and fear, I nodded and said, "Yes, please."

Delighted by my response, Adam led me toward the door that Zane was still studying intently. When we approached, he turned his attention to us, his eyes going to Adam's. There was a silent exchange before Adam stopped us, allowing Zane to go first. We were next but I stopped us.

My eyes locked with the floor and I swallowed thickly. This was it. I was about to leave the tower. The tower that had been my home for I didn't know how long. A part of me didn't want to leave. I was used to it here. I knew what to expect. Out there, in that world that was all metal and loud, I didn't know where I belonged or if I'd belong anywhere. I knew I belonged here.

"What's wrong?" Adam asked.

Licking my lips, I lifted my gaze to Adam's concerned eyes. "Nothing. Just...let's go." I gave him a small smile, forcing myself to take that first step into the stairwell. The twins brought up the rear as we descended the set of stairs. My feet burned from the cold of the stone, but there was nothing I could do about it now.

The stairs curled around the interior of the tower and it was quickly discovered that there were no other windows in the tower, leaving us in pitch darkness.

"Hold on," Zane called back at us, and then a moment later a soft, yellow glow filled the stairwell.

We continued down the stairs for a few moments, my nerves jerking up and down the closer we got to the bottom. After we had been heading down for a few minutes, Luke leaned over my shoulder, "So, what do we call you? Rapunzel can't be your name."

I glanced back over my shoulder into his pretty eyes that were even more golden in the yellow light. He really was attractive, but he had a point.

What was my name?

My eyebrows scrunched together as I thought about it. The fog on my mind had begun to clear ever since they had appeared. When the cuffs had come off, it was like a veil had been lifted. I still didn't remember how I ended up in the tower or how long it'd been, but I did know one word. One that stuck out above all the others.

"E-Eva," I stuttered out. "I think my name is Eva."

Chapter 3

My discovery was short lived, because the roar of voices was even closer now than before. Ahead of us, another door like the one above came into view. We must be at the bottom of the tower. The prospect thrilled and terrified me all at the same time. I tightened my grip on Adam's arm, causing him to smile down at me.

"Well, Eva—if that's your name," Blake snorted. "I hope you're ready for this, because like it or not, you're now a celebrity."

I didn't have a chance to ask him what he meant by that before Zane pushed the door open and bright sunlight came beaming down on me. Eyes squinting, I held a hand up over my eyes. Besides the sun, there were flashing lights causing spots to fill my eyes. Adam dragged me closer as if trying to protect me from those lights.

The voices were becoming more distinctive now as we drew closer. There were too many people for me to pick out one person, but they all wore strange clothing just like my saviors. Except they were also shoving metal objects toward our faces, floating orbs hovering above their heads. They were like the little eyeball I'd seen upstairs, watching my every move.

I turned my face into Adam's arm, trying to hide my eyes from the flashing lights. It didn't keep them from trying to talk to us though.

"Master Adam, Master Adam," one voice shouted, getting their metal stick close to us. "Who is this woman? Did you find her in the tower? Where did the tower come from?"

"Is this a ploy to add to your campaign as Arch Mage?" another one asked, making me wonder once more about those words. Blake had said them before too. Was Adam their leader?

Blake shoved the reporter back and growled, "No comment."

"Is she human?" A man who didn't seem to get the hint jumped in front of us, not caring that the others were glaring holes into him. "Will she go to the reeducation center? How will this affect your run for Arch Mage?

Will Arch Mage Heizer have anything to say about it?”

This time, it was Zane who stepped in front of us. That kind expression of his turning to the man. Placing a heavy hand on the man's shoulder so that the cross around his neck swung from side to side, Zane calmly stated, “All questions will be answered as they are known. Please respect our privacy.”

The man stared at Zane as if he were the scariest and most beautiful thing he had ever seen. I wasn't sure what he saw in the gentle man's face, but I made a note to be careful around him.

When the man moved out of our way, the rest of the crowd opened a path for us. Zane's stepping in didn't stop them from asking their questions, but they at least stopped trying to block our path.

“No comment,” Adam kept responding with a flat stare. Those two words didn't stop them from asking questions I didn't know the answer to. It also didn't deter the people, though they followed us as Zane and the twins helped clear a path for us.

The area surrounding the tower was not pleasant looking. Dead trees and plants littered the area. Markings decorated the hard ground and stone, creating a walkway.

I didn't have time to check much more out before my rescuers were ushering me into some sort of metal contraption with wheels.

The door shut behind us, making me jump in the leather seat. I scrambled to the window as Adam took the seat beside me, and the others crammed in on the other side, so they faced us.

I didn't know why I was so panicked, but suddenly I had to see the tower. My hands pressed against the glass, my nose squished up as I struggled to see the tall stone obstacle blocking out the sky. It was hard to believe this had been my prison for who knew how long. It was all I'd ever known. All I'd ever understood, and I wasn't sure if leaving was going to be a good thing or if I was just opening myself up for a lot more torture and pain.

My view of the tower was blocked out as the metal box was surrounded. The people with the sticks and floating balls crowded around the box, pressing their faces against the darkened windows. Then, suddenly, we began to move. I fell back in my seat, bumping into Adam, whose arms wrapped around my waist. I clung to Adam as Luke chuckled.

"Never been in a car before, huh?" His eyes sparkled with mischief. "I can't wait to get you on my motorcycle." The wicked grin on his lips told me I was not going to like whatever a motorcycle was, though I was tempted to find out.

"Uh, okay..." I drew out and then glanced back out the window. A car. Hmm. There were more of these cars passing by us as the car moved toward whatever destination they had in mind. I hoped it involved somewhere that didn't move. My stomach was starting to churn.

Adam huffed as if my answer amused him, drawing my attention back his way. He twisted his wrist and some red swirls appeared, startling me. Out of nothing, a beat-up book appeared.

I stared hard at his hand, wondering where the heck the book came from. At first, it wasn't there, and then it was as if by magic. Ha. I giggled. Magic. As if that were something new to me. From Zane's observation, my whole being had been preserved by magic. Not that I'd known it at the time, but it shouldn't surprise me now.

"Do you like to read?" Adam asked, peering over his book, that from here I could see had a shirtless man embracing a big breasted woman. What kind of story could be in there?

Confusion caused my face to scrunch. "I'm not sure. I'm not sure I even can read." Pure frustration filled me as I realized I didn't know much of anything.

"Of course not," Blake scoffed, crossing one leg over the other. "You're a human. Humans are filthy scum who only care about eating, fighting, and fucking. Though you might like that trash Adam reads."

"Blake!" Zane clucked his tongue and shook his head. "Such language in front of a lady."

I smiled softy at Zane while Blake scowled, and Adam made an offended whine.

"Hey." Adam clutched his book to his chest with a hurt expression. "It's not trash. It's art."

"Art my ass. And she's not a lady." Blake gestured toward me with a disgusted sound. "She was locked in a tower that until five hours ago didn't exist."

Didn't exist? I glanced around me at the others, looking for an explanation. How had my tower not existed until a few hours ago? I knew I'd existed longer than that...hadn't I?

Zane was the first one to notice my distress.

Leaning forward, Zane patted my knee. "Don't worry about him. He's a bit testy because his trials are coming up."

I didn't know what kind of trails he was talking about, but nodded anyway. Chewing on my lower lip, I struggled to ask about the tower. I wasn't sure what kind of person I used to be, but the one I was now didn't want to be a bother. They'd saved me after all.

"You're wondering about the tower, aren't you?" Zane smiled kindly, a knowing look in his eyes.

Shyly, I bobbed my head.

"Well, it was the funniest thing. We were doing our daily rituals when we were called in by the council." I must have looked confused, because he added, "The Council of Mages, which is what we are." He circled his hand around the four of them. "We're mages. Which is complicated to explain right now, but I promise to circle back around to it later." The gentle expression on his face made me feel at ease, knowing he would do as he promised. "Anyway, your tower appeared in Old Central Park—that's where we were—just completely out of nowhere."

"It was crazy!" Luke bounced in his seat, excitement lighting his face. "We seldom have anything this awesome happen. At least, not in this part of the country. I mean, there was that dragon that got loose, but that was up in Canada, but you're our first mystery."

Confusion and embarrassment caused me to shift in my seat. I didn't want to be anyone's mystery to solve. At least, not until I solved it myself. Blake's words about me being in that tower for a reason was all too clear in my head. Who knew what they would do if they found out that I deserved to be there? What would I do? Probably run as fast and as far as I could.

"We need to make a plan before we get home." Zane shifted over to meet Adam's gaze. "Not to be offensive...but what are we going to do with the lovely Eva?"

Blake's single golden eye narrowed on me. "Send her to the reeducation center. That's where she belongs."

Luke smacked his brother on the shoulder. "Don't be such a dick. We can't send her there. We have to find her family." Both of his golden eyes slid over to me and his lips pursed. "Do you have any family?"

I blanked. Shaking my head from side to side, I winced as my hair pulled from the gesture. I lifted my butt and pulled my long hair into my lap. I slid the strands between my fingers over and over. "I don't know. I don't think so..."

"That's alright, we'll put a notice out to see if anyone can claim you." Adam looked up from his book, placing his hand on mine, and squeezed my fingers.

"And if no one does?" I chewed on my lower lip, glancing down at my hands.

"Then you can stay with us!" Luke exclaimed, before anyone else could answer. I lifted my eyes from my lap to meet his eyes, smiling slightly.

"No, she can't." Blake jumped in right after. "We don't need any humans in our household. We do fine on our own."

"Oh, come on," Luke whined, shoving his brother with his foot. His white robe fell open and my eyes strayed to his exposed chest. Something pulsated between my thighs and for some reason my face heated.

Adam gave me a knowing wink and then leaned close to me, so our shoulders rubbed against one another. A sizzling tingle buzzed through me at the touch and I flushed harder.

"Adam, tell my idiot brother that she can't stay with us," Blake growled, his eyes flashing in anger, then his voice lowered. "We have sensitive events in progress that we cannot have some random, lowly human snooping around." His eyes lingered on me with growing revulsion.

The blond man next to me shifted to face me, still holding his book in his hand. "Eva, will you tell our secrets?"

My mouth opened slightly, and then I clamped it shut, shaking my head. "No."

"See?" Adam turned back to his book and shrugged a shoulder. "She's fine."

"That doesn't mean crap. She could be lying. You can't know that," Blake snapped, throwing a hand in my direction. "For all we know, she's a spy for Master Tuck."

Luke snickered. "Yeah and I'm a hippogriff."

"I can make you a hippogriff." Blake tensed, his fingers coming up and making purple wisps in the air. The air in the car thickened and I reached for Adam's arm, my fingers digging into his shirt sleeve.

My eyes darted between the twins, wondering what was going to happen. Could Blake turn Luke into a hippo-whatever he said? However, neither Zane nor Adam seemed worried. In fact, they seemed to act like it was a normal occurrence.

"We're here," Adam announced while I fretted over the twins, closing his book with a snap, the red wisps taking the book to wherever it had come from.

The car stopped, jerking me out of my seat. I fell forward into Zane's lap, my hands reaching out catch myself on his legs. Blushing brightly, I pushed off him, but not before noting how muscular his thighs were.

"S-Sorry," I stuttered out.

"Not a problem, it was an accident after all," Zane said calmly, but for some reason, I felt as if he was laughing at me, which only made me mad. I couldn't help that I didn't know anything. Or that the car would launch me when it stopped. I was getting tired of being the butt of their jokes.

"Are you ready?" Adam offered me a hand as Zane helped lift me from the car floor. "The horde hasn't caught up with us yet, but it won't stay that way forever."

"The horde?" I asked before I could stop myself. I really should just keep my mouth shut. The more I asked, the dumber I sounded.

"The horde," Luke answered this time, shutting the car door behind us, "is the group you saw back at your tower. They chase after us mages like flies on shit—I mean crap. Sorry." He gave me a sheepish grin, rubbing the back of his head.

"It's fine." I shook my head, my long hair swaying around me like a curtain. I think a haircut might be on my list of to-dos. I wiggled my toes on the hard slab. And shoes. Shoes were a must.

"Come." Adam took me by the elbow and led me up to a gray building. It was almost as tall as my tower, with several rows of windows. On the side of the building was a big red symbol—a branch shaped into a cross. The doors we went through moved on their own and people rushed around so quickly, I worried that if Adam didn't have a hold on me, I might have gotten run over.

"We need to see a healer," Adam told the woman behind the desk.

The woman was about mid-forties, her hair curled into tight, brown curls on her head. She didn't even look up from what she was doing, but pushed a square-shaped object with a shiny black surface toward us on the counter. "Fill out this form and sit over there." She pointed a finger over to an area where at least twenty or more people waited in different states of need.

"Why are we even here?" Blake frowned, his eyes following mine to the other people. If anything, he looked even more disgusted by them than me.

Adam ignored Blake, keeping his eyes on the woman. He didn't take the square but pushed it back across the table. "I'm sorry, I don't believe you understood me. We need to see a healer *now*." He had a charming yet deadly grin on his lips that made a chilling thrill go down my spine.

It had quite a different effect on the woman when she finally looked up. The irritated frown on her face fell, and whatever rude words I felt she had prepared promptly died on her lips. She took the square back, barely able to breathe let alone get her words out.

"M-Master Adam. I do apologize. I didn't see you there." She stood from her seat and grabbed something off the counter in front of her. "I'll get you Healer Marsh right away." She turned away from us and started speaking rapidly into the black object in her hand.

"Don't be frightened." Adam placed a hand on mine, his eyes squinting at the sides as he smiled. "These people just need to be shown who's boss."

"And Adam loves to flaunt his notoriety around." Luke clapped a hand on Adam's shoulder with a teasing flash of his teeth.

"I do not." Adam pushed Luke's hand off his shoulder and shifted his clothing back into place. "This is an emergency."

"Sure, and scaring that poor woman was necessary." Zane rolled his eyes but grinned as well.

"No, that was just fun." Adam chuckled with his friends and then turned as the woman returned.

"Healer Marsh is with another patient right now, but he said to show you to the back, and he'll get to you in a moment." She bowed her head several times as if afraid that Adam might smite her for making him wait.

Grinning like a fiend, Adam said, "Excellent. Show the way, my good lady."

Chapter 4

The woman nodded eagerly and rounded the counter, taking us through a pair of double doors.

The ground was cool and shone slightly as the light bounced off it. My nose wrinkled as the scent of some strong chemical hit my nostrils. I glanced around to see if any of the others noticed, but none of them seemed bothered.

There was so much noise. Even here inside the building. There was never silence. Not like in my tower. Outside, there had been the people, animals, and what I now knew as cars constantly chattering in my ears. Inside this place, which I could only assume was a healing facility, there was a constant buzzing and beeping coming from even more objects I didn't understand with shiny, reflective screens. Some of the screens had numbers and letters on them. Some only had wavy lines. But all of them made some kind of noise.

I lifted my hands to my temples and tried to push back the oncoming headache. I'd wanted to feel something—well, now I was getting a sensory overload.

We passed several doors and people. Some of them were dressed like Luke, in white robes, and others were dressed in various styles and colors. There didn't seem to be one set type of clothes that everyone wore. It made me wonder why they chose to wear such extravagant garbs. Of course, I only had my plain white dress so I might be a bit bitter.

"Here we are." The woman stopped before a door, a nervous smile on her lips. "The best room in the whole hospital."

Zane and the twins ushered me into the room as Adam spoke to the woman in hushed tones. I turned my head from the large, stark white room with a bed and table, and tried to crane my head to see what Adam was telling her. The way she curled into herself as if she was trying to make herself as small as possible made me think whatever Adam was telling her wasn't something nice.

In the end, she gave a sharp jerk of her head and then scurried away. Adam turned from the hallway, closing the door behind him. When he saw me looking, a genuine smile pulled at the edges of his lips. "We won't be disturbed now. Feel free to lay down." He gestured toward the bed and I grimaced.

"I'll stand." I shifted away from the bed, my hands touching the wall behind me. The surface of the white wall was cool to the touch, making my back jerk away from the burning sensation.

"I don't blame her." Blake sniffed. "If I'd been locked up like that, I wouldn't want to lay down for a week, maybe even a year." He shook his head and briefly I could see beneath his dark locks to the eye beneath. Dark purple, a shockingly different shade than the gold of his other eye, glinted at me. As if noticing my stare, his eyes jerked up, glared at me, and then turned away to the window.

What was that?

I didn't have time to find out or ask before there was a knock on the door. Stiffening against the wall, I waited for the knocker to enter.

Luke was the first to greet the man who entered, a great big grin on his face as he pulled the man into a hug. Wearing similar white robes as Luke, I was beginning to think he might be the Healer Marsh that the woman had spoken about.

"Healer Lucas, you could have done a better job than I ever could," Healer Marsh admonished, the kind-looking older man shook his head.

Luke ducked his head and smiled. "I know, but you have so many more resources than I do back at the house. Besides, we wanted to make it all official and everything. You know how the council gets."

"Do I ever!" Healer Marsh chuckled, and then glanced over at Adam. "And you, did you have to give my receptionist such a hard time? She's only doing her job."

Adam crossed his arms over his chest and stared him down. "I did nothing of the sort."

Healer Marsh only shook his head and laughed. His eyes went around the room, nodding as he greeted Zane and Blake. When his eyes landed on me, he arched a brow. "And who might this be?" He moved toward me, his hand outstretched, I was assuming to shake hands, but when he came within a foot of me, he jerked his hand back, a disgusting sneer covering his face.

"A human. Why would you bring a human here?" Healer Marsh's eyes shot to Adam, accusation in his gaze.

"What of it?" Adam stated more than asked. "She's under my care, I'm not about to take her to one of those crap human doctors."

"But to bring her here?" Healer Marsh shook his head. "I've never had a human walk through my doors, ever."

"Then this will be the first," Adam snapped, grinding his teeth together. "Or I'll take it up with Arch Mage Heizer, who appointed me to this mission."

"And what mission would that be?" Healer Marsh questioned, curiosity now replacing his abhorrence.

Before Adam could answer, the door opened once more to reveal another man I didn't know. Well, I didn't know any of them, but there was starting to be a few too many men in this room. In any case, this one had a head full of gray hair and a long beard, his mustache curling down around his plump lips. He wore a dark emerald robe with gold lining and a long necklace. At the end of the necklace was a circle surrounding a branch, kind of like the one I'd seen on the side of the hospital.

"Master Tuck," Adam greeted the man with a suspicious frown. "What are you doing here? Arch Mage Heizer assigned this task to me."

I still didn't know what task he was talking about. Was I the task or was it the tower? Or maybe something else altogether.

Master Tuck either didn't care or was ignoring Adam's irritation. He pushed his way into our little circle and stopped right in front of me. His eyes moved over me in such an intense way that I wanted to crawl back up in my tower just so his beady little eyes wouldn't find me.

"So, this is the girl," Master Tuck muttered, tapping his lip with his forefinger.

"How do you know about her?" Luke asked, closing the distance between us, so he stood by my side. I was happy for the support, but wasn't sure what he could do against someone I assumed was a higher rank than him. No one was going around calling him Master anything.

The older mage shot Luke a patronizing look before saying, "I have eyes, and you weren't exactly discreet in your exit from Old Central Park." He shot a chastising look at Adam who didn't so much as flinch. "Everyone in the Northern Hemisphere knows about the girl." Master Tuck turned his gaze back to me, leaning forward slightly as if to inspect me better. "The question is, who are you and what were you doing in that tower?"

I swallowed hard, my eyes darting to the others for help. Thankfully, one of them heard my plea, because Zane moved in on my other side.

"Master Tuck." His calm voice made my shoulders loosen immediately. Was it just me or did Zane have that effect on everyone? When Master Tuck shifted back from me, his expression softened, but was no less intense. So, it wasn't just me.

"Cleric Zane, I have to say I didn't expect to see you here." He tilted his head slightly to the side. "I would have thought you were still buried in the church with your books."

Zane chuckled politely. "Yes, I do have quite a lot of work to do, but it is also my duty to keep watch over Master Adam. We know how impulsive he can be." Zane slid a sideways glance at Adam, who had pulled his book out of nowhere again and was completely ignoring us.

"Yes, that he is," Master Tuck chuckled as well and then frowned. "What do you make of this..." He leaned toward me again and took a big whiff. "Human? She's human?" His bushy gray eyebrows shot up into his hair.

Nodding, Zane placed a hand on my shoulder. "This is Eva. She was locked up with a stasis spell and..." He trailed off, his face scrunching up in frustration. "A few others that I will have to do some research to figure out."

"But why would they lock up a human?" Master Tuck clucked his tongue and stared at me as if I might have the answers.

Believe me, I wished I knew. I would love nothing more than to know why I was in that tower, or for that matter, who I was. However, the longer I was here and the less people who liked the aspect that I was human, the more I worried what I might find out and more importantly what they would do with that information.

"The better question," Adam said, his book snapping closed, "is why hide her prison?"

There was silence for a moment, all of them deep in thought. Except for Blake. Blake was too busy boring holes into my skull with his eyes. Why did he hate me so much?

When he noticed me looking, he shook his head and turned his face back to the window. The others seemed to come out of their thoughts at that moment as well. Without warning, Master Tuck reached for me, which made the rest of them move as well, Adam's hand getting there first to stop him from touching me.

"What is the meaning of this?" Master Tuck cried out, trying to shake his hand from Adam's grip. "She is the property of the Mage Council. She should be taken to Headquarters immediately."

I shrank back from his grip, not wanting to go with him. I'd only just met him and already didn't like him. I'd rather take my chances with the four men who saved me from that tower. Though, saved might be a strong term for it depending on how this all turns out.

"No, she won't." The finality in Adam's voice made Master Tuck blanch and then his face turned a weird shade of red-purple. His interference made my shoulders sag and a sense of relief fell over me. Before Master Tuck could argue in return, Adam's hand landed on top of Master Tuck's. With a tight grip, he threw Master Tuck's hand off me and stepped between us, blocking me from Master Tuck's view. "I was assigned this task. I will see it through." Master Tuck made a strangled noise like he wanted to interrupt, but Adam didn't allow it. "And I will see it through however I see fit. Currently, I think it best Eva see the Healer before we take her back to our home."

The prospect of going to the four men's home made a flutter of excitement fill my stomach. Really, anything not my tower would have made me happy at that moment, or so I told myself. It couldn't certainly be the chance of being around the mages who saved me. Not possible. Right?

"Your home!" Master Tuck cried out the same time Blake said, "Our home?"

"Yes." Adam's head shifted to look at Blake, giving him a warning look that had him clamping his mouth shut, but his expression didn't soften. "Our home is the safest place in Neo New York for her right now. At least until we figure out what and who she is. If you have a problem with it, take it up with Arch Mage Heizer." I didn't have to see his face to know he had a dangerous look in his eyes. He had used it once already with the receptionist, and by the sound of his voice and the look on Master Tuck's face, he was using it now.

Making a sort of choking sound, Master Tuck seemed like he wanted to argue, but then took a deep breath and huffed, spinning on his heels and leaving, the door slamming behind him.

"Childish," Blake commented at the closed door, and then rounded his glare at Adam. "What did you mean she was going home with us? You can't be serious. We don't know her. She could slit all our throats in our beds."

"Yes, I am." Adam turned slightly so I could see the grin on his lips. He shifted so he was facing me and said, "That is if that's okay with you?"

My eyes slowly lifted to Adam's and then shifted to Blake who looked like he wanted to slit my throat right then and there. My gaze moved to Luke, who was seconds from bursting with excitement and it made me smile. Zane had a serene sort of expression on his face. When I searched his face for any kind of refusal, he just nodded.

Turning my attention back to Adam, I inclined my head briefly. "I'd like that."

Blake let out an irritated huff while the others cheered and talked all at once. Healer Marsh, who I had forgotten about until this point, interrupted them.

"Well, then I better get started. I'm sure you all want to get home." The way he said it made me think more that he wanted to be done with us as quickly as possible. It was solidified when he gestured for me to sit on the bed, careful not to touch me at any point.

My body sank into the soft mattress and my feet came off the ground as I sat down. Chewing on my lower lip, I watched Healer Marsh, nervous about what he might want me to do. Or what he could possibly do to me.

"Relax." Zane placed a hand on my back, startling me as I twisted my head to see him. I hadn't heard him move behind me at all. His hand did calm me down in some way. I wasn't sure if it was just Zane himself or if he was using some sort of magic on me.

"Now, I'm going to check your vitals," Marsh Healer explained with a little less vexation in his voice as if he were falling into a normal pattern. He held up a tan bracelet shaped object and slid it over my wrist, being careful to touch me as little as possible. "This device will monitor your heart rate, check your blood pressure, and scan for any abnormalities you might have. Now that I think of it..." He tapped his lip and frowned. "We really should have you quarantined until we know for sure you don't have any contagious diseases."

My shoulders bunched up at the thought of being caged up again. My heart raced, making the bracelet on my wrist beep rapidly as the numbers on it rose in digits. I tried to scratch at the device to get it off, but I couldn't remove it.

"You're going to break it," Healer Marsh chastised. "Just let it do its job." To Adam, he said, "I can get the paperwork drawn up to check her in and then we can reevaluate in a few days if she is safe to be around other—"

"Absolutely not," Adam interrupted Healer Marsh with a stern glare. "There is no obvious threat, and by the reports on your own device, she has no abnormalities."

"But it's procedure to—"

"No, I won't hear another word about it." Adam held his hand up, not letting the man speak anymore. "I will take full responsibility for her. Besides, if she does have any contagious disease, I will be the first to know." His face softened and a playful smile with a sharp edge found its way onto his face.

Healer Marsh visibly gulped and then nodded. Turning back to me, he no longer spoke as he continued writing down a few things on another shiny black window. When he was finished, the men led me out of the hospital and through a door opposite of where we came in, probably to avoid the horde.

As I sat in the car once more, I pulled my bottom lip between my teeth, worrying it while I looked around me. These people were as much a stranger to me as anyone, but they seemed like the better option than going with Master Tuck or quarantine for that matter. I didn't like the way Master Tuck had looked at me, as if I were something he could use. For what, I wasn't sure, but I think Adam was right. The safest place for me was with them. At least, for now.

Chapter 5

I must have fallen asleep in the car, because when I opened my eyes, I wasn't where I was when I closed them. As I shifted in place, I realized I was in a bed. A soft, fluffy cloud of a bed with lavender sheets and a matching canopy above me.

My eyes felt heavy, and everything in me screamed to go back to sleep, but my curiosity won out in the end. Sitting up in the bed, I scanned the room. It was by far bigger than my tower, but then again, most things were.

My mind shifted back to the fact that I wasn't where I fell asleep. Who had put me here? The blond-haired man named Adam flashed in my mind. Had it been him? He seemed the most likely of the men who had saved me. The redhead with the strange eyepieces on his nose might have done it, but from my first impressions of him, Zane seemed more interested in the spells on my binds than me.

The twins were something else altogether. If they really were twins. I never got a proper introduction. Luke, the one with nothing but smiles for me, could be described as a happy puppy wanting nothing more than to play with the new toy. His counterpart, Blake, would be more likely to toss me out of the tower window than tuck me into bed. A bed that was far nicer than anything I was used to. Since the only thing I had in comparison was the tower stone floor, my expectations weren't that high.

Beside the bed, I had a small table with ornate golden handles. On top of it sat a glass. I picked it up and took a drink. Water. When was the last time I'd tasted water? Or anything for that matter? As if my thoughts were the trigger, my stomach grumbled in protest.

Food. I could eat now. My mouth watered at the prospect of having real food in my mouth. I'd stopped dreaming about food a long time ago. I couldn't die of hunger or thirst, so wanting those things had seemed pointless.

If someone had asked me what the first thing was I wanted to eat when I got out of my tower, I couldn't tell them. I didn't know.

My brain was still cloudy and when I tried to remember things, it made my head hurt. I supposed a positive about not knowing anything about myself was the ability to find out everything all over again. Perhaps before I didn't like kiwi and now I would like it. Who knew? Certainly not me.

The thought of food urged me to get out of bed. My feet landed on the plush furs spread out on the ground, my toes wiggling in it for good measure. There were some things I was sure I took for granted before. Now, just feeling anything on my feet beside the cold tower floor was enough for me.

There were so many things I could do now, things I wanted to do. Eating was obviously high on the list, but a hot bath was a close second. I searched for the bathing area, but didn't see any sort of tub in the room, but that didn't bother me. The moment my eyes found the glass doors leading outside, I couldn't stop my feet.

I wanted to be outside. I'd been inside for so long nothing could deter me from just sitting out in the sun all day long and inhaling the fresh air. It had to be far better than the stagnant contents of my tower. Healthier too.

My hands turned the handles, and I almost sagged in relief when they opened easily. Shoving the doors open, I stepped out of the room and onto a metal platform hanging on the outside of the building. My lips pressed together tightly as my eyes scoured the sky. My brows furrowed at the dull, grayish-blue with hardly a cloud.

This wasn't right. I might not remember much about my past, but I remembered the sky. Bright blue with sunlight beaming down on me. I had longed to have the same light warm my skin, the wind to blow through my hair when I finally escaped my tower. This wasn't what I imagined at all.

My nose wrinkled as the smell of the world around me assaulted my nose. Too many smells to register just one, but it was an overwhelming putrid smell that had me plugging my nose just so I wouldn't vomit. The stench hadn't been this bad back at Old Central Park, as they called it, or even the hospital. Maybe the air was worse the higher up you were?

The sounds registering in my ears distracted me briefly from the smell. The loud booms, that incessant buzzing, and people chattering down below me. I placed my hands on the railing and leaned as far as I dared. The platform was nowhere near as tall as my tower, but it would hurt if I fell. Now that I had my freedom, death was not something I was willing to embrace. Not anytime soon, in any case.

There were men and women dressed in elaborate clothing like those who rescued me. They hurried along the sides of the streets. Their heads held high, not paying any mind to those they forced to move out of their way. Those who moved were not dressed so nicely. Dull colors of browns and gray covered their forms, they kept their eyes down, and quickly ducked their heads and darted out of the way of one of the ornately dressed.

Curious. It seemed social classes—something I surprisingly still remembered—were still an aspect of this world. Something I would think with all their knowledge of the mystics they might have grown in other ways as well. It seems I was wrong.

I took a few deep breaths of the air and coughed. Racking, choking gasps that had me rushing inside and closing the doors tight. Not even the air we breathed was the same. What has happened to this world?

I shifted across the room, needing something to take my mind off the heavy thoughts. I glanced around the room and found a door to my left. Walking toward it, I opened it to reveal a large tub and privy.

They had a room specifically for cleaning and relieving one's self? Curious.

Moving into the room, my eyes trailed over everything I could find. There was a mirror in here, as well as some plush cloth sitting on a metal shelf. The privy was far shinier and smelled nicer than my mind recalled. It was interesting to find out that I remembered far more than I thought I did as I discovered things.

I shifted away from the privy with its weird scented water in the hole and a loud rush of water startled me. Grabbing at my heart, I stared at the privy hole as the water swirled around inside of the seat. Frowning, and wrinkling my nose, I moved away again. Only for it to make the loud noise once more and the water swirled. With a grin and a giggle, I did it twice more, coming close and then moving away, delighted when each time I did the water moved around in the bottom.

Bored with that, I moved to the tub. Shiny silver knobs were attached to the sides with a long spout coming out of the wall. After fiddling with a few things, I figured out how to get the water out. I pushed a button on top of the spout and shrieked as freezing cold water sprayed out of some contraption from above, soaking me and my clothing through.

Backing quickly away from the tub, I swiped a hand over my face, pushing my wet locks out of my eyes. I watched the water pour out from the top for a few moments, confusion filling me. Determined to get clean, I inched toward it and angled my body around the spray before pushing the button once more. To my relief the water stopped pouring out of the top and changed back to the bottom, but now I had another problem.

The water wasn't staying in the tub. It all kept going down a hole in the tub. Who would put a hole there? Was I supposed to clean with only an inch of water?

Figuring I would have to make do, I dragged my wet dress over my head and dropped it to the floor. I stepped into the tub and shivered as the cold water touched my feet. Baring my teeth, I found a bottle of pretty scented liquid that I poured generously into my hands and washed as quickly as possible. I leaned toward the spout and splashed it over my body, trying my best to get it clean.

My hair was a growing problem that frustrated me to no end. It was so long I had to use the entire bottle of soap to clean it all, and then trying to get it rinsed out had my back aching and my body shaking with chills.

Deciding I was clean enough, I jumped out of the tub and turned the water back off. I grabbed a fluffy cloth nearby and dried myself and as much as I could of my hair. Wrapping another cloth around myself, I made my way back to the bedroom.

Looking around for something else to wear, I found a dresser and mirror sitting off to one side of the room. I hadn't seen myself in forever. Did I still look the same? I hadn't thought to look in the bathroom. Too interested in getting clean, but now I had no reason not to look.

As I approached the mirror, my heart began to race. I stared down at the ground until I stood in front of the reflective glass. With a shaky breath, I lifted my gaze and landed on the familiar figure looking back at me. Letting out a heavy breath, I didn't realize how relieved I would be to see my face, unchanged by the time.

After a moment of staring at myself, taking in every familiar feature, I grimaced. The cloth I had wrapped around myself fit my slightly curvy form well and was a large improvement from the dress I wore in the tower. Still, my hair was a wet, tangled mess stuck to my face, neck, and shoulders as it brushed the floor. The face I remembered, but the hair? What kind of person was I before to want hair this long?

Determined to chop it off, I dug through the nightstand and then through the dresser. Not finding anything I could use, I pulled out the first thing I found, a sky-blue dress that laced up the front. When I dropped it over my head, the sleeves sat off my shoulders, exposing my neck and collarbone.

A bit more exploring led me to find a piece of fabric that I couldn't quite figure out what it was for. I held the scrap of cloth up, its three holes not making much sense. Was this for my head or maybe a shirt? I tilted my head to the side as I tried to figure out what I had in my hand.

"That is a pair of underwear."

I spun around to see Luke standing in the doorway, a bright blush on his face. Glancing back to the garment, I said, "Underwear? What are they for?" I dangled it out to him with one finger, which only made him blush harder. Why was it so embarrassing for him to see?

Stepping further into the room, Luke took the piece of fabric from me and held them out so that the two smaller holes were pointed down. "You put your legs in them, and they go up over your..." He trailed off, his eyes going to the junction between my thighs.

My eyes widened as I realized what he was thinking of. "Why would I want to wear those? They don't cover...anything."

Luke shrugged, avoiding my gaze, his face turning an even brighter red. "Well, you don't have to, but some find them comforting."

"Why?" I blinked up at him innocently.

"Because it creates a barrier between your...your, you know, and everything else." He glanced up at the ceiling and scratched the back of his head. "Please, don't make me say it."

"Say what?" I smiled, realizing how uncomfortable this was for him. Did he not talk to women often? Maybe he hadn't been with one? It would explain why he couldn't talk about female anatomy.

Luke's eyes jerked down to meet mine. When he saw me smiling, the embarrassment disappeared from his face and a pout appeared. "You're so mean. How can someone so pretty be so mean?"

I giggled, covering my mouth with my hand. "Sorry, I couldn't help myself."

"Here." Luke held out the underwear to me with a sourpuss frown.

Cocking my head to the side, I smirked. "No, thank you. I don't need them." I found a pair of soft, flat shoes next to the dresser and slipped them on. Somehow, they fit perfectly, and a part of me wondered if someone had been fondling my feet while I slept. I turned back around to see Luke gaping at me.

"You don't..." Luke trailed off, seemingly unable to finish the sentence as I walked back toward the door, a grin on my lips. "Now, hold on a moment."

"What?" I shrugged, leaving the room. I didn't know where I was going, but my stomach demanded food, and I would find it. "You said some like it. I don't see the point of them."

Blowing out a hard breath, Luke shook his head. "Never mind. Can we change the subject? Talking about what you are or aren't wearing this early in the morning is not good for my heart." He clutched a hand to his chest, and I giggled once more. He was a funny one.

Chapter 6

We walked down the hallway with Luke pointing out different rooms. The library, a few offices, as well as a multitude of bathrooms. They even had an area with strange metal stands with black circles on them, and another with a large pond in the house. Something that fascinated me.

"How do you have a pond in your house?" I gaped at water through the large window that spanned most of the wall. My fingers touched the glass as I pressed myself to it. An image tickled the back of my mind of water splashing back and forth, giggles and laughter turning into moans of pleasure as a man with bright blue eyes smiled at me.

"It's a pool not a pond." Luke chuckled beside me and the image drifted away. I glanced his way with a small smile. "Do you know how to swim?"

I pulled my lower lip into my mouth and thought. "I'm not sure. Maybe?"

"Would you like to find out?" Luke asked, taking my hand and drawing me toward the glass door leading into the pool area.

Happy to find something out about myself, I let him lead me until my stomach rumbled, reminding me of my first mission. "And where is the kitchen?"

Luke seemed startled by my request, but then nodded profusely. "Of course, I'm sure you're starving. You haven't eaten since..." He trailed off as if expecting me to fill in the blanks for him.

Narrowing my eyes, I said, "I don't know any more than you do, so you might as well get it through your head." Not from the lack of trying. I wished I remembered more than I did. It would have made things a whole lot easier.

A bit dejected, Luke tucked his hands into his pockets, pushing the opening of his white robe wider. He seemed to like that outfit. He wore the same thing the day before. Then again, I'd been wearing the same dress for who knew how many years. I wasn't one to judge.

"You know, you're quite a bit more talkative today than yesterday." He led us around a corner where a delicious smell wafted out, making my stomach growl.

Quickening my feet toward the smell, I said, "I don't know. I feel different."

I really wasn't sure what to tell him. It was like a veil had been taken off my mind, and I could finally think freely. I didn't know what kind of person would come out now. I was just happy to be able to think for myself.

"Different how?" Luke asked, as we walked into what I could only assume was a kitchen, but it was nothing like any kitchen I'd ever seen.

"I don't know, just better," I murmured, too distracted by what I was seeing.

Blake leaned against a counter in the middle of the room, a cup in his hand, and his single, visible eye down on one of those square things like the receptionist had tried to give us. Zane stood by a large silver square box. His red hair braided down his back. Fire burned beneath a pot and the delicious smell coming from it made my stomach cry out. Another silver box, this one with doors, stood partly open, a light shining out of it. As I rounded the counter, I could see different boxes and jugs sitting on their shelves.

"Good morning, Eva," Zane greeted me with a smile, a large black spoon in his hand that he occasionally used to stir whatever was in his pot.

The figure inside the door tensed and straightened up from where he had been looking. Bulging muscles twitched beneath a sleeveless brown top as the owner slowly turned around. Black hair moved with him, his brown-black eyes locking onto my face. His own face was covered from nose to neck, only allowing me to see the top half of his face. Those eyes—the way they slashed into me—was enough to let me know that he didn't like me.

"This is Gage, he's an assassin," Luke explained, offering me a seat on the opposite side of the counter from Blake. The latter promptly glowered at me before going back to the square. Ignoring the nagging need to find out why the dark twin hated me so much, I accepted the warm cup from Zane.

A booming timber came from the large beast named Gage. "That's confidential."

Seeing him full on now, I had to say I was a bit intimidated. I'd thought he had muscles before, but those were just small ones compared to the large pecs and thick thighs beneath his formfitting, pocket covered pants. A black tattoo wound up his wrist from one of his gloved hands to disappear beneath his shirt. It seemed to be a lizard of some sort, but not any I'd ever seen. What kind of lizard had wings?

Luke's chuckle pulled my eyes away from Gage, who stared at me like he knew I had been looking. Luke threw an arm around my shoulders. Apparently, it wasn't only his healer part that made him not care about boundaries. "This is Eva. She doesn't know anyone but us, not even herself for that matter. Who is she going to tell?"

I grimaced, but it was true. Besides Healer Marsh and Master Tuck, the men before me, including Adam who hadn't yet appeared, were the only ones I knew. On top of that, I wasn't sure what I'd even do with the information I had, let alone use it against them.

"That still doesn't give you the right to tell Gage's secrets," Blake said, giving Luke a warning look. What kind of secrets were they hiding? I glanced at the two of them, searching for what they might be keeping from me.

"Are you brothers?" I blurted out. Blake and Luke stared at me for a moment, so I kept going. "I mean, you look alike, so I automatically guessed you were twins, but I don't want to make assumptions."

Suddenly, the room filled with masculine laughter, making my face heat and body tingle in delight. Luke bumped his shoulder against me and grinned broadly. "How'd you guess?"

I wasn't sure if he was teasing me or being serious. Deciding he was making fun of me, I huffed. "I just met you all. It wouldn't be right for me to make assumptions."

"You're right," Zane nodded, a bit ashamed. "We shouldn't tease you. I apologize."

Blake snorted. "If she can't handle a bit of teasing, she's in the wrong household." He shot me a mean look. "Maybe you'd be better back in your tower."

At his words, my chest tightened, and panic spread through me. I shook my head and backed away from the table. "No. No, please no."

Seeing my reaction, Blake's expression fell. Luke reached out and took my hand, pulling me into his embrace. His hands rubbing up and down my back. Warmth spread across my body and I was on the verge of passing out, so I didn't have the energy to push him away.

"It's alright, Eva," Luke murmured into my hair. "Ignore Blake, he's only kidding. You won't ever go back to that tower. I promise."

A harrumph from Gage pulled my eyes away from Luke's shoulder. "Don't make promises you can't keep."

Luke drew back from me and glared at Gage. "I don't. And you shouldn't assume the worst of people right from the start. I know your job makes you a bitter and suspicious dick, but for once could you lighten the fuck up?"

My eyes widened at Luke's sudden outburst. He really didn't want anything to happen to me. Which meant he would also keep me from going back to my tower. All at once, I felt safer by his side.

"Well, this is a happy conversation to be having this morning." Zane sighed, rubbing his eyepieces on a cloth he pulled from his pocket. "What a good impression we are making on our guest."

"Don't worry about me." I tried to reassure him with a weak smile. "I'm easily distressed it seems."

"And as you should be." Zane nodded, putting his eyepieces back on his face. "Who knows how long you've been in that tower? It would only make sense for you to be distraught over the idea of going back. Blake shouldn't have threatened you so." He gave Blake a chastising look, causing the dark-haired twin to duck his head and scowl.

I moved away from Luke and back to the counter. I might think I'm ready to be out of my tower, but I obviously needed to take things one step at a time. My mind busy, I picked up the cup in front of me and took a drink. I swallowed despite myself, making a face. Ew. Bitter.

Zane chuckled and pulled something out of the box behind Gage. "Here, try this." He poured a white liquid into the black in my cup and then stirred it with a spoon. The drink turned a light brown color, and I tentatively took another drink. This time, instead of bitterness, there was only sweetness.

"That's so good," I exclaimed, taking an even bigger drink. "What is it?"

"Coffee," Zane answered with a smile.

A snort was followed by Adam entering the kitchen. "That's not coffee. That's flavored milk." He winked at me and then pushed a button on a black device sitting on another counter. Putting a cup beneath it, black liquid like mine spewed into the cup. When it was done, he held it up and took a drink. A hum of pleasure came from him that made my toes curl. "Now that is coffee."

Rolling his eyes, Zane picked up his pot and brought it over to me. Luke placed a plate in front of me before Zane plopped a yellow substance with red, green, and pink bits in it. Picking up the fork provided, I didn't even stop to ask what it was before shoveling it into my mouth.

Instantly, a low moan slid from my mouth as I closed my eyes. So good. I couldn't remember the last time I ate. To taste something other than my own saliva was utterly divine. I scooped up another forkful and lifted it to my mouth. Another delicious bite. A throat cleared, and my eyes popped open. Five sets of eyes stared at me as I chewed what I decided were eggs.

"What?" I asked, swallowing hard, and like that, the spell was broken. Blake snatched up his square and stomped out of the room. Gage pretended to be interested in something on his arm. Luke and Zane turned to make their own plates. Only Adam didn't look away, lifting his cup up to his mouth, his eyes sparkling with amusement.

"So, Eva," Luke said, clearing his throat as he took the seat next to me. "After we eat, I thought I would check your vitals once more, you know, since you said you felt different today." I arched a brow, my mouth busy chewing, and Luke quickly added, "You know, just to be sure." His cheeks pinking at my stare.

"Okay," I answered, taking a drink of my milk flavored coffee. I closed my eyes briefly at the wonderful taste and decided I would always drink my coffee this way.

"Then afterward." Luke chopped up his eggs, picking out the tiny green bits and setting them to the side. "We can show you around the house. We want you to feel as comfortable here as you would at your own home."

My expression dropped at his mention of home, causing Zane to make a noise in his throat. Luke glanced over to Zane and then to me, his face flushing. "I mean, not that you remember what your home was like but...ugh. This is too hard." He threw his fork down and slumped in his seat.

Adam moved over to lean across the counter from me, a soft grin tugging at the corner of his lips. "I think what our friend here is trying to say is that we want you to feel safe and to think of our home as yours."

Nodding, I gave them each a pleased look. "I understand and can't be more grateful for what you have done for me. You rescued me from the tower and now are letting me stay with you. I couldn't begin to repay you."

Gage made a noncommittal sound and Adam straightened, his face smoothing over. "Well, you just worry about getting better.

Maybe you'll remember something. I'm sure you had a family who would be worried about you."

While I finished my food, I thought about Adam's words. Did I have family around still? It didn't seem likely. I knew I had been in that tower far longer than just a few years. Things were still blurry, but some things I didn't know before were coming back to me. Nothing substantial, just little things. Things I didn't know until after the fact.

Like coffee. Until I drank it and heard the word, I didn't know if I liked it or not. Now having just tasted it, the memory has crept to the surface.

I never used to like coffee, and my favorite fruit was bananas. Now, if I could only upgrade that to who the heck I was and why I was in that tower, then everything would be peachy.

"Now, tell me if anything hurts," Luke explained as his hands hovered over my form. We were still sitting in the kitchen, except the food had been cleared, and the others had left to do whatever it was they needed to do. I sat perfectly still in my seat while Luke did his little examination.

"What's that over there?" I stared at the silver box the pot still sat on.

Luke paused his examination to look where I did. "The stove."

"And that?" I moved my gaze to the large one with doors.

"The refrigerator. It keeps the food cold." He frowned. "Haven't you seen one before?"

I lifted a shoulder. "Not that I know of."

Without me asking this time, Luke gestured to the one Adam had gotten his coffee from. "And that's the coffee machine. The microwave. And this..." He picked up the black square with the reflective screen. "This is the com system. Whatever you want to know, you can find it on here. Well, most things." He placed it in my hands and touched the screen, bringing it to life. "You can make calls." When my brows furrowed, he added, "Talk to other people and send messages. Lots of things."

I held the device in my hand, touching different things on the screen as Luke turned his attention and hands back to my body.

A warm sensation moved over me, and I shifted in my seat. Luke moved his hands over my face, down my neck, and over my chest where he paused for a moment. My breasts, having a mind of their own, decided at that moment that they were cold. Luke's golden eyes widened, and a faint blush covered his cheeks. I'd never known someone who blushed so much. It was adorable really.

"Uh, um. I think you're okay." Luke dropped his hands and turned his face, so his hair fell over the majority of it.

"Okay," I said, hopping off the seat. "Anything else?"

Shaking his head, Luke cleared his throat. "Uh, no. But, uh, are you not … you know, wearing a bra as well as underwear?"

"What's a bra?" I cocked my head to the side.

Luke lifted his hands in front of his chest, cupping them as if he were holding melons before him. "Uh, you know, a brassiere. They cover your … your breasts."

I glanced down at my chest. "I have a dress on, why do I need a bra?"

The healer seemed utterly at a loss. He stumbled over his words all while trying not to make eye contact with me. "They make it so that your... your..." He moved his hands in front of my chest, pointing at my nipples.

"My nipples?" I cracked a grin. "What? Do they offend you in some way? Do you not like nipples? Or do the women here not have them?" The more questions I asked, the brighter red Luke's face became.

"No, no. I l-like nipples. I mean, no I don't like...I mean. Ugh!" He threw his hands up in the air and stomped toward the door just as Blake entered.

"What's his problem?" Blake asked, bypassing me and going for the refrigerator. He pulled out a cylinder and popped the top, taking a deep drink from it.

I shrugged. "He doesn't like my nipples."

Blake spat out his drink and coughed, hitting his chest repeatedly. I rushed over to him, smacking him on the back. He pushed me away with a glare.

"He doesn't what?" he croaked out, setting his container down.

Frowning, I gestured toward my chest. "He doesn't like my nipples and says I need a bra or something to cover them up." Immediately, Blake's eyes dropped to my chest, and then he looked away quickly, a faint coloring to his cheeks. Apparently, he was a blusher as well.

"Well, it is unusual for you to go without one, but it is entirely up to you." Blake picked up his container again, taking a small sip. He shifted slightly, his hair moving enough for me to see the purple eye.

Without meaning to, I stepped toward him, my hand reaching up to brush the hair back from his face. Blake froze in place, his eyes on me as I pushed the hair back. One gold and one purple eye stared down at me.

The purple eye's pupil dilated, and my fingers traced a long scar that went from the top of his cheek to his forehead, marking across the eyelid.

"What happened?" I asked in a soft voice, as if talking about it were taboo. I shouldn't have said anything, because Blake knocked my arm away from his face, causing the hair to cover the eye again.

"Don't touch me," he spat, before storming out of the kitchen. I seemed to be making a lot of people do that lately.

Sighing, I glanced around the kitchen. I'd seen my room and the feeding area, but not the rest of the house. Since no one was around to show me, I guess I would have to figure it out on my own. A low pressure reminded me of my other bodily needs.

I pressed my legs together, my head shifting from side to side. Exploring would have to wait until I released my bladder.

Chapter 7

After I relieved myself in one of those new fancy toilets, I strolled through the halls. The place was so huge, I wouldn't be surprised if I ended up lost. Really, it would be no one's fault but theirs if I stumbled into somewhere I wasn't supposed to be.

Curiosity had me peeking in every door I came to. None of the doors were locked or very interesting. Most were bedrooms. Some were office-like areas. There were more washing rooms than I ever thought necessary. Who needed to go that often?

While I contemplated the oddness of it all, I came to a stop before a set of double doors. They were made of a pretty wood and had intricate flower designs with colorful glass windows. I pushed one of the doors open slowly, peeking my head inside.

Real flowers, mostly varieties of roses, filled stone pots along the sides of the room.

Benches made of the same stone sat on either side with a path down the middle. I slid between the opening of the door and into the room, hoping I wasn't disturbing anyone. As I made my way down the long path, my eyes moved up to the columns holding a glass ceiling up.

Made of the same colorful glass as the windows in the doors, these were placed in the form of a picture, a woman reaching up to heaven while a white-winged man held his hand out. I remembered something about religions, God, and angels. Though a memory tickled my mind as I knew I'd never been a big believer myself.

I sniffed.

Look where that had gotten me. Locked in a tower and no memories. Maybe if I had prayed more in my past life, I wouldn't have ended up there. Then again, I wouldn't be where I was now. With five attractive and mysterious men wanting to help me.

It could be worse.

Smiling to myself, I lowered my head from the ceiling. At the head of the room sat a large stone cross that came up to my waist with the same branch I'd seen everywhere engraved into the center of it. Stepping closer, I traced my fingers along the image, the red of the branch deeply cut into the stone.

"Are you a believer?" a low, raspy voice asked, and my head jerked toward the sound of it.

Off in a corner, hidden by the shadows, sat a figure. They inhaled and then the red tip of something glowed in the dark. Smoke billowed out of the man's mouth before he stood up and moved into the light.

Clutching my hand to my chest, I let out a heavy, shaky breath. "Zane, you scared me." I gave him a relieved smile as he approached me, but as he came closer, it fell. Something was different about him.

Not wearing his glasses, Zane had his hair loose from its braid and it hung down over his shoulders. A tattoo peeked out from the left side of his shirt, which had been unbuttoned to mid-chest, I could just barely make out a circle and the points of a star. The strange glint in his eyes made my feet move backward on their own.

"You didn't answer my question," Zane stated, his hand holding the stick he had been smoking. He flicked the end of it, sending ash to the ground. Placing it back into his mouth, it barely hung between his lips as he spoke. "Are you a believer?"

"Uh, I..." I glanced at the cross and then back at him. "I don't know. I mean, I don't remember." I winced as my back touched the rose bush, the thorns pricking my skin. Glancing back, I turned and then ended up on one of the seats.

Zane closed in on me, propping one leg up on the stone bench beside me. This was not the same man I'd just seen in the kitchen. There was no soft smile for me. No gentle hand to help me up. He had a darkness to him that I couldn't describe. Not to mention the salacious way his eyes roamed my body and his finger coming out to trail across my collarbone. I held back a shiver.

"You should believe," he said finally, drawing in the smoke before blowing it into my face.

Coughing, I waved a hand in front of me and glared. "I don't know who you are, but I'm not going to play your games." I tried to step over the bench and leave, but he caught my wrist, pulling me over the bench and across his lap.

"Don't leave so soon. We were just getting to know each other." The wicked grin on his lips made my skin crawl, and I struggled against his embrace. The burning stick in his hand lingered over my skin like a threat, and I forced myself not to move.

Something in the back of my head told me not to struggle. That struggling would only excite him further. I didn't know where I knew this, from but I took it to heart.

"What do you want to know?" I demanded, my eyes skittering to the stick and back to him. "You want to know if I believe? Well, I don't. How could I believe in a God who would leave me to suffer alone? The days begin to blur together after a while," I found myself saying, the grin on his face morphing into something more of a curious nature. I didn't know where the information was coming from just that it kept coming out of me. "I'd long since stopped counting by the tenth year. The hundredth. How could I believe in a God who would do that to me? What did I do to deserve such a punishment?"

"What indeed?" The Zane creature leered down at me as his head dipped down toward mine. I scrunched my eyes closed, not wanting to see him if he was going to kiss me.

Suddenly, I was jerked from his arms. A large bicep wrapped around me, pushing me behind an even larger figure. Gage stood in front of me, the tattoo on his arm pulsating as his muscles tensed.

"You shouldn't be here," Gage said, and at first, I thought he was talking to me, and then I realized it was Zane he was talking to.

The Zane figure smirked and shrugged. "The cleric let his guard down. Who am I not to take advantage?"

"A demon is who," Gage growled, and I stared at Zane in awe. There was something inside of him? No wonder he wasn't acting his usual self.

Gage pulled something out of his pocket, a smaller version of the cross and branch on a beaded chain. The creature in Zane flinched back and frowned. Taking a drag from the stick, he flicked it to the ground before stepping on it.

"Fine. I'll leave," he told Gage, but then grinned wolfishly at me. "If you'd have prayed to me, I'd have never left you alone." With those final words, he threw his head back and laughed. Energy moved through the room, causing the hairs on the nape of my neck and arms to stand up on end, and then Zane collapsed to the ground.

Gage moved away from me, kneeling next to him. He lifted Zane's head into his lap and dug into his pants pocket. Withdrawing Zane's glasses, he placed them on his face and then promptly smacked him on the face.

Ouch.

Zane jerked up with a yell. Jumping to his feet, his hand on his face, Zane frowned at Gage. "What was that for?" His eyes then took in my quivering figure, and shame filled his face. "It happened again, didn't it?"

"Yes," Gage answered, his eyes narrowing. "You must be more careful."

Sighing, Zane sat down on the stone bench near him. Dropping his head between his arms, he leaned on his knees. "I was being careful. Or I thought I was, I guess I kind of got distracted…" His eyes moved from the ground to where I stood.

Feeling it was safe to approach now, I sat on the bench across from him. "Are you okay?"

"I'm fine." Zane's brows rose in surprise. "I should be asking you that. He didn't do anything to you, did he?"

I shook my head. "No, just said some things." I paused and pressed my lips together tightly, trying not to ask about what was obviously a touchy subject, but I couldn't help myself. "What was that?"

"A possession," Gage answered, his arms crossed over his chest, his form looming over us menacingly.

Zane's brow creased further. "What he said."

"I don't understand." I glanced between the two of them. That voice in the back of my mind reminded me what that word meant. Demons were things of fairy tales. Things that the priests used to keep the people in line. Surely, they weren't real? And it was inside of him? "How did that...demon get inside of you?"

Zane straightened and pushed his glasses back up his nose. "The magic we mages use can be dangerous if not handled well. I specialize in spell casting, as you know, and sometimes those kinds of studies lead to dark places. When I was younger, I was a lot cockier than I am now." He offered me a guilty smile, but I honestly couldn't imagine a cocky Zane. He was too soft and gentle. Nothing like the creature I'd been greeted by earlier.

"When we mages come of age, we must go through a ceremony, a ritual that shows what power resides within us. I thought I was far more experienced than I was and attempted a spell that would have made me the most powerful spell caster in the world." He wiped a hand over his mouth and gave a bitter chuckle. "That was if I hadn't completely botched it."

I placed my hand on his and nodded for him to continue. Taking the comfort, I was offering, he placed his hand on top of mine, his fingers stroking my knuckles. Warmth spread through me where he touched me.

"The spell was to call a demon from beyond the veil and bind him to a talisman, so I could call upon his powers when I needed them." He lifted his other hand, pulling the side of his shirt back so I could see the tattoo beneath. "This tattoo was supposed to appear on the necklace I had picked out to be the binding object, but somehow, a piece of me ended up on it, and instead of binding to it, the demon bound itself to me. Unfortunately, my great plans to use his powers backfired, and now it is me who is being used."

"Hence why he needs to stay on his guard." Gage glared down at me as if it were all my fault. From the way Zane kept peeking up at me, it probably was.

"I'm sorry." I pulled my hand back and rubbed the back of my neck. "I didn't mean to be a distraction."

"No, no." Zane shook his hands between us, his eyes widening. "It's not you. I promise. I've been working too hard lately, and that combined with the recent events, I just haven't been as careful about keeping my guard up."

"Oh," I breathed out, not quite believing him.

It seemed I was causing everyone all sorts of trouble. I hadn't even figure out the whole problem with me being a human thing yet. Just my being here seemed to be an issue. In other situations, I might have been flattered that I was causing all kinds of mayhem for these men. I'd seen the way they looked at me. Well, except for Gage and Blake who looked more like they wanted to shove me back up into my tower. But Zane, Luke, and Adam were all attracted to me. Not that I wasn't feeling the same way. I just didn't want to be a bother for those who saved me. After all, they could just as easily put me back where they found me.

Zane clapped his hands together and stood up. "Well, that's enough seriousness for a while. Perhaps you would like to see the library?" He offered me his hand, and without hesitation, I took it. Lifting me to my feet, he ushered me out of the room. "Maybe we can find something about your tower. Or maybe even you. Have you remembered anything yet? Maybe a surname?"

Shaking my head, I clutched his arm tightly. "No, not really. I'm getting some things, but mostly likes and dislikes. I know I was in the tower for a long time but how long?" I lifted one shoulder and let it drop, not filling him in on what I'd told his other self. Best to keep them in the dark until I knew for sure. "Your guess is as good as mine."

"It might be better that way," Gage said, coming up behind us. "Some things are best left forgotten." He moved past us and down the hall in the opposite direction.

As Zane led me away, I couldn't help but wonder if Gage was right. Was my past something I really wanted to know? What if what I found was worse than not knowing at all? A gnawing, sinking feeling settled in my stomach, making me wish I knew just what I was getting into.

When we arrived at the library, Zane pushed the door open and led me inside. Dozens of shelves were filled to the brim with books and scrolls.

Several soft looking seats were spread out through the room, as well as a few tables. A few of the tables had some of those com systems on them, but they were larger and were a rectangle shape. I stared at them as we walked by and Zane stopped us.

"You're probably wondering what this is, huh?" He smiled softly and then reached over to touch the shiny black surface. "It's called a computer, much like the smaller versions you've already seen. You only have to touch the screen to find what you want. There's a voice command system as well, but I've always had an issue getting it to understand what I'm asking." His brows furrowed adorably before he continued, "But in any case, you can find a lot of useful things on there. Recipes, news, you can even watch television." It was my turn to look confused. "That's where people act out stories for your amusement."

"So, like a play?"

Zane's eyes lit up, the gold flecks in his hazel eyes really shining. "Yes, exactly. You're remembering things. That's wonderful." He grabbed my hand in his, squeezing it slightly before drawing me away from the tables. "But I think what we need won't be on there. A lot of chronicles of spells and judgments were still written down on paper a few hundred years ago. You might be able to find something here."

I followed him as Zane began pulling books from the shelf and handing them to me. Once my hands were full, he took one look at me and took them from my arms, placing them on a table for me to get started on. While he went back to the shelves to find more books, I perused my findings.

"History of the Mage Council," I read aloud, opening the book and flipping through the pages. The fact that I could read the language was a life saver. It would have been difficult to get anything done if I was illiterate.

"The Mage Council was formed during the fifteenth century after the fall of Necronite." I frowned at the word 'Necronite.' There was no definition for it. Holding my place in the book, I glanced at the others on the table. My hair caught underneath me and with a frustrated growl, I gathered it up and twisted it over my shoulder. I really did need to cut it already.

"*The Rise and Fall of the United Nations. The Great Collapse of the Americas. How to train your human?*" The last one I made me scoff and toss it aside. What exactly were they training me for? I was a person, not an animal who could be given a treat every time they did a new trick.

After going through all the books and not finding anything on Necronites, I stood and went in search of Zane. He had been gone for quite a while. How did anyone expect me to figure anything out if they kept leaving me on my own?

I glanced down the aisle in search of the redheaded man, but he was nowhere to be found. I rounded the last shelf and found Adam and Gage arguing in hushed tones. Gage's back was to me, hiding me from Adam's view. Jumping back behind the shelf, I peeked between the books.

I really shouldn't be eavesdropping on them. It wasn't right. These men had been nothing but kind to me, and what did I do? Disrespect their privacy.

Still, regardless of my own chastising thoughts, I stayed and listened. Perhaps I wasn't that good after all.

"You had no right to bring that thing here," Gage growled, pointing a finger at Adam's chest. "You put us all at risk with your recklessness."

Thing? Was he talking about me? It made me like the giant man a little less.

Adam didn't seem intimidated by Gage's large form at all and simply laughed. "I don't need your permission to do anything. I was assigned this mission from Arch Mage—"

"Heizer, I know," Gage snapped. "That doesn't mean that you can do whatever you want. You should have given her to Master Tuck when you had the chance."

"But he would have taken her to one of those facilities, you know that," Adam scoffed, leaning back against the table next to them. "You know what they do to humans there. I couldn't bear to see her dissected and used for parts." He frowned and stared down. "She's more than that."

"Better her than you." Gage grabbed Adam by the arm, forcing him to look up. "You are only a week away from them announcing the new Arch Mage, and if you still want that to be you, then you need to get it together. A woman, especially a human woman, is not a complication you need right now."

Adam jerked his arm out of Gage's grip. "Don't you think I know that?" He moved away from him and started to pace. "Don't you think I realized that this might have been a ploy by Tuck all along to distract me?"

"He is your only opposition," Gage reminded him.

"And all the more reason to keep her out of his grasp. If he is using her to get to me, then I want to know why before he can put his little plan in motion." He sighed and dragged a hand over his face. "It's also just as likely that she is an innocent bystander in all this and doesn't know what the hell is going on."

Gage scoffed, "Hardly. She's already causing a rift between the five of us. Zane shifted today."

"What?" Adam gaped, his eyes hardening. "When did this happen?"

"Not thirty minutes ago. He was this close to taking a bite out of your precious human." Gage held two fingers up, squeezing them together until there was barely an inch between them.

Adam rubbed his chin, his face deep in thought. "That is a problem."

"Exactly," Gage announced, throwing his hands up. "We should get rid of her now before it gets any worse."

"No, no." Adam shook his head. "It only means we need to find out who and what she is sooner. Most importantly, why she was in a tower hidden in the middle of Old Central Park."

"There you are!" Zane cried out from behind me, I jerked around, my eyes wide at being caught. "I've been looking everywhere for you."

"I was looking for you too," I rushed out and forced myself to calm down as a set of boots pounded toward us. Gage and Adam appeared behind Zane, Gage with a suspicious glare and Adam with a disappointed one. Trying to throw them off their suspicions, I explained, "I was reading that book *History of the Mage Council,* and it mentioned Necronite, but I couldn't find anything that said what it was."

Adam relaxed slightly, but Gage still watched me intently. I had a feeling he didn't quite buy my story. Moving away from the shelves, I approached Zane. "What's a Necronite and why did it fall?"

Zane chuckled, adjusting his glasses behind his ear. "Necronite was a meteor. It fell to Earth about, what, the fifteenth century?" He glanced at Adam and Gage who nodded in agreement. "It caused a great wave of magic to spread through the world, which, as you can imagine, caused quite a lot of panic." Zane led me out of the bookshelves and back toward our table, all the while talking in my ear. "Shortly after its fall, the time we now know as the Dark Ages began. Many mages went into hiding after that."

His words faded as I glanced over my shoulder at Adam and Gage who hadn't followed. Gage's eyes were still on me, but Adam's were lower, a lot lower. A warm tingle in my cheeks started before Gage smacked him on the back of the head. Holding back my giggle, I forced myself to pay attention to what Zane was saying and not what I'd overheard. Whatever Gage or Blake thought, at least I knew Adam was in my corner.

Chapter 8

After staring at what seemed like hundreds of books, Zane brought me to what he called the living room. There was an even larger version of the computers in here, except he called it a television. What the difference between this and the computer was, I didn't know or ask. There was too much information to process today. My brain was overflowing with information.

Luke was already there, sitting on what they called a couch. His top robe was lying on the side of the couch, his feet propped up on the low table in front of him. His golden eyes were intensely focused on the screen before him.

Curious to see what they were so absorbed in, I shifted closer to the couch, my eyes on the images before me.

"Monica, I can't live without you," a handsome man announced, pulling a dark-haired woman into his arms. He gripped the back of her head and pressed his lips to hers. They kissed for a moment before the woman pulled back dramatically.

"We can't, Theo. What would your brother think? After all, I'm pregnant with his baby," Monica exclaimed loudly, all the while clutching him to her.

Luke made a startled sound and shifted in his seat. His eyes were locked fully on the screen. I was tempted to wave a hand in front of his face to see what he'd do.

"But it's not his baby, Monica," the handsome man, Theo, declared, and then stared off into the distance. "For it was me who snuck into your room that night."

"You?" she gasped, her hand going to her mouth in horror.

"Yes." Theo kicked his chin up in a strange movement. "You are pregnant with my child."

The screen went black, and then a person came on the screen wanting to sell us the new and improved Shake Maker. My eyes pulled from the screen to Luke, who jumped up and shouted, "Oh, come on. You can't leave us hanging like that."

I moved further into the room and sat on the edge of the couch next to him. "You must really like that story." I smiled at him inquisitively.

"Oh, yeah." Luke nodded, sitting back down. "It's the best. But they always leave you with a cliffhanger before the next episode. I swear that's how they get you to keep watching."

"You like it, don't lie," Zane commented from the other room. A moment later, he entered with a tray of glasses and a pitcher of pink liquid. "Would you like something to drink? After all that studying, I'm sure you're exhausted."

I accepted the glass and took a sip of it. Finding I liked the sweet and tangy taste, I took another drink. Downing the cup, I ducked my head at the bemused look Zane and Luke were giving me.

"Another?" Zane asked, holding the pitcher up.

"Yes, please." I held my cup out for him to fill back up.

When he was done, I settled back into the couch to watch the show with them. It was amusing to see Luke get so excited about imaginary people. He would shout and jump at the expected moments in the story. In between breaks, Luke caught me up on the storyline. Apparently, the show thrived on drama and the most ludicrous scenarios.

Who would really mistake someone's brother for their lover?

"Ick, you're watching this crap again." Blake appeared out of nowhere. He literally wasn't there and then he popped up on the edge of the couch. He scoffed at the show, but the moment the commercial was over, his eyes were glued to the screen.

I exchanged a look with Luke, who rolled his eyes and pointed a thumb at his brother when he wasn't looking. I covered my mouth to stifle a giggle. Apparently, it didn't go unnoticed because Blake shot me a rude look before shooting up and going in the other room.

"Why does he hate me so much?" I questioned, unable to hold it back any longer. "I mean, I haven't done anything to him. Have I?" I tried to recall if I'd offended Blake in some way since we met, but seeing as it had only been two days, I was coming up blank.

"Nah." Luke shook his head. "It's not you. Blake's always like that." He picked up his glass and took a drink but didn't set it back down. His hands clasped around it as he stared at it, dark thoughts on his face. "When we were kids, he was better. Nicer. But as we got older and we both started to study our separate magical arts, he became distant." He looked up from his glass and smiled sadly. "I mean, we're still pretty close, but not like it once was, not since..." He trailed off, but didn't finish it. "Anyway, don't let it get you down. Just breathing offends him."

"And lettuce," Zane added.

"And people who chew too loudly," Adam said, poking his head out of the kitchen.

Luke grinned back at him. "Oh, yeah and dogs. He hates dogs."

Adam and Luke exchanged a wicked look which made me want to ask what happened, but Gage's presence killed any words on my tongue. At first, he seemed like he was about to say something and then he saw me. He clapped his mouth shut and headed straight for the kitchen. Did I stink? Did I have some kind of disease? It was beginning to feel that way.

"Don't mind him either," Luke poked me in the arm. "He doesn't respond well to females. Like ever."

"Now, that's not true," Zane interjected and then his brow furrowed. "Okay, so the non-four-legged variety doesn't really count, but I swear he's had a girlfriend at some point."

Luke snorted as he stood up. Taking my glass from me, he offered me a hand up as well and started for the kitchen. Apparently, it was the designated feeding time, which was fine by me. My stomach grumbled its agreement.

As we stepped into the kitchen, Adam looked up from where he stood by the stove. "Hey, Eva, do you know how to cook?"

"Uh, no. Or I don't know." My face scrunched tightly in concentration. Skills like that, I didn't have a clue if I could do. I mean, I knew how to go to the bathroom. How to put my clothes on. How to have sex. Or at least, I thought so. I wasn't exactly sure if I'd ever had sex before. And now I was thinking about sex in a room full of men who I was deeply attracted to.

Thankfully, none of them were paying any attention to my face, because I was pretty sure I was blushing. Luke and Blake were talking about the show, Zane was looking at one of those computer things, and Gage was glowering...at me. Turning my attention away from him, I moved over to where Adam stood.

Glancing over his shoulder, I watched as he put things into a pot of bubbling water. He noticed me watching and handed me a knife.

"What?" I asked, blinking at the knife.

"Want to dice those tomatoes?" He gestured toward four large tomatoes next to a wooden board.

I took the knife that he was offering and moved over to the board. Staring down at the tomatoes, I tried to decipher how to go about cutting them. What exactly did 'dice' mean?

"Are you sure it's a good idea to arm her?" Blake snarked from the middle counter. "You know, she might just be waiting for her chance to sink that knife into your back."

Frowning at his accusation, I forced myself not to turn around and confront him. Just ignore him. He doesn't mean anything by it. I kept repeating that to myself, more for Luke's sake than Blake's. I could happily see myself shoving the knife I had into his back.

"Do you want some help?" Adam's voice brushed against the side of my ear, making me jump in place.

Spinning around, I swallowed thickly and nodded. "Yeah, that'd be good."

Moving behind me, Adam slipped his arms around me. A snicker came from the group behind us, but I couldn't focus on them. All I could think of was the warmth of Adam's chest pressed against my back. His hands covered mine and arranged the tomato and knife into the right position. He put pressure on my hand holding the knife, and I pushed down, slicing the tomato. We cut them into circular slices and then strips before finally small cubes. The entire time my heart was in my throat and my body flushed with desire.

"There we go. All done," Adam murmured in my ear, but then just like that, he was gone.

I turned in place to see his back to me, his attention on the stove. Feeling like I'd walked through a desert and hadn't had a drink for ages, I moved to the other side of the counter, searching for my glass. Luke had brought it in, and someone had refilled it. Drinking deeply from it, I stared down at the counter and told myself to calm down. Adam didn't think of me that way. I'd heard it myself. He was only nice to me because he wanted to find out if I worked for Master Tuck. Which I didn't. I'd disliked that man on sight. Even if I had the choice to work for him, I wouldn't in a million years.

"So, did you find anything useful in the library today?" Luke asked, thankfully making me think of something else.

I shook my head. "No, nothing that tells me who I am or why I was in the tower. I did learn a bit more about the mages." I tapped my cup against the counter and chewed on my lip. "What I don't get is why you hate humans so much. Why are they lesser? Just because they don't have magic? That hardly seems fair."

"Well..." Zane looked around the group and then cleared his throat, clearly uncomfortable. "We don't hate them per se."

Blake scoffed, "Speak for yourself."

"Anyway..." Zane shot Blake a warning look. "It's true that when the Necronite fell, magic came to the Earth, transforming select humans into mages. At first, there were more humans than mages, but then as the years went on, they began to war with each other. We mages tried to stay out of human affairs as much as possible, but eventually, there weren't very many of them left and the world was—"

"Shit," Gage interrupted. "The world was utter shit. That's what humans did to it. They fought and polluted until there was nothing left." I stared at the large, quiet man, the words he said the most he's ever said to me personally. Watching him talk was so interesting. With the mask over his lips, it made him seem so much more mysterious. It made me wonder what he looked like beneath the mask. Did he have a scar or an ugly face?

"So," Luke started, interrupting my thoughts as he rubbed his hands together in front of him, "we mages stepped in, sort of took over. We reorganized the government. Got rid of the military and changed a lot of the rules. As you can imagine, the humans were pissed." He snickered and then cleared his throat when the others gave him a horrified look.

"But mostly scared," Gage added, his arms crossed over his massive chest, making his muscle flex. I took another drink of my cup, clearing my throat. "Fear makes people do stupid things." He shook his head as if he knew a thing or two about those kinds of things.

"Exactly." Zane pointed at him, before looking back at me. "So, while I hate to put it this way, there really isn't another way to say it. We had to put the humans in their place. We had the power and they didn't. We were, are, more powerful than them and they hated us for it. So, in a way, they made themselves the lesser class." He shrugged at the end as if that made it somehow better.

"That doesn't tell me why I shouldn't be in your house," I mused, reminding them of the conversation with Master Tuck. "Just because I'm human? Should I be in my own part of town or something?"

"No," Luke chuckled, placing a hand on my back as if it would comfort me in some way. "Nothing like that. It's just that most humans go through schooling on how to serve the mages. It's our way of giving them a place in society that doesn't allow them to cause destruction like they did before."

"Serve like how?" I shifted away from Luke's touch as Adam started to hand out plates.

"For example, you would have cooked this meal," Adam explained, scooping a pile of noodles onto my plate before topping it with the tomatoes we'd cut earlier, which he'd made into a sauce.

"Hmm, well, I'm not above cooking for you, it's the least I can do really, but I'm afraid my skills are not quite up to edible level." I spun my fork in my noodles, scooping them up before putting it in my mouth. "I mean, this is great." I chewed it up and swallowed it. "I mean, I couldn't even cut tomatoes right."

Adam grinned mischievously. "Don't worry, I think we can find something around here for you to do." The way he looked at me made my whole body warm again.

"Come on, Adam." Zane bumped him on the shoulder. "Stop teasing her. We have a meeting after dinner. So..." He picked his plate up and mimed eating.

I wasn't sure what other things the humans had to do, but if it was anything like

the things running through my head, then
they were some really lucky humans.

Chapter 9

I sat in a chair, a maid behind me braiding my hair. A smirk sat on my lips as I stared at my own reflection. No one was more beautiful than me. Or more powerful.

The maid placed a circlet on my head, a white diamond with a red branch embedded in the middle of it. She bowed, and I waved her away with a sneer.

Standing up, I smooth my glittering silver gown over my curves, a body many men have died for. Have given up their kingdoms for. My beauty was the only thing I held dear to my heart. No one and nothing else mattered.

Sure, I'd found comfort in men's arms before, but they were passing amusements. A means to slake my lust and nothing more. They didn't make me truly happy. No, the only thing that would do that was revenge.

Revenge on those who had denied me what I deserved, who destroyed my family because of their own lust for power. Well, I would show them what it meant to be strong. What it felt like to have their lives in the hands of someone else and beg for it as I squeezed.

Yes, they would pay. They all would.

"My Lady." The maid came back, dipping in the doorway. "They're ready for you in the church."

"Fine," I snapped, giving myself one more look over before grabbing the bottom of my wedding dress and whipping around. I passed by the bowing maid and walked down the hallway. Servants scurried to move out of my way as I stormed past.

Vermin. They were all vermin. Bottom feeding creatures not worthy of my attention.

I could hear the rustle of unsettled guests before I even reached the chapel. They think I didn't know what they whispered. Selfish. Cold hearted. Evil incarnate.

Witch.

They didn't know how close to the truth they actually were. For years, I have passed under the radar as a simple human. Biding my time until I could find a way to the top. Now that I have won the heart of the king, I would set my sights on the Mage Council next. They were guiltier than any of the pathetic wastes of space here, and when I ruled, they would all bow to me, an abomination. That's *what they called me before they cast me out. Well, this abomination has claws, and was going to make them pay for what they did to my family and me.*

Setting my revenge aside, I put all my attention on the doorway before me. Archways of flowers, roses of white and red, decorated the entryway to the chapel. A carpet of deep red sunk slightly with each step I took. Flowers petals from the flower girl littered the ground before me.

I didn't wait in the doorway. I didn't have a father to give me away. Nor did I hold a bouquet of flowers. They would just turn to ash beneath my raging emotions. I'd be lucky to control my powers with my new husband, let alone the foliage. I forced my face to smooth over, to hide the deep-seated hate in my heart as my groom came into view.

King Midas. The richest and most powerful man in all the lands. He had been so easy to entice. So desperate for someone to fill his lonely heart. I only had to offer him a listening ear and a peek at my cleavage to gain his affection.

He was only a stepping stone in my plan. He didn't deserve to be in my presence, let alone touch my heart. Him or his sniveling daughter. I refrained from sneering as my eyes landed on the dark head of hair standing next to her father.

Only seven years old and yet she held so much power in her father's court. That would change as soon as I was made queen. Children should be seen and not heard, and this one had a particular penchant for getting her father to bow to her every whim. A smirk tugged at my lips. Well, not anymore. The only person King Midas would be bowing to would be me.

The people made the appropriate noises as I passed them. I let their praises wash over me, like a waterfall of power. If I didn't have any magic at all, then this might have been enough. Their adoration and love, it was almost more powerful than the abilities I'd been blessed with. Almost.

My feet stepped up onto the small stage where the cleric waited. His robes were white and red, the branch on my circlet embroidered on his chest. The mark of the mages. A secret mark that the humans knew nothing about. They thought it was just some religious symbol used to differentiate us from other factions. They couldn't be more wrong.

This was the first time I'd ever worn the symbol in public, the first time I'd screamed from the rooftops that I was one too. The widening of the cleric's eyes made my heart pound in excitement. He wouldn't give me away, but I had no doubt that as soon as the wedding was over, he would scurry off to tell the rest of them.

As I said my vows, I smiled. To others, it might look like I was overjoyed to be getting married, but if anyone dared to look deeper, they would see the fire in my eyes. For there would be a raging inferno that would engulf this land and its people as soon as the mages were mine.

So, run, little man. Tell your masters I'm here. Tell them their queen is coming for them.

I sat up in bed, my heart pounding in my chest. What the hell had that been? The dream had seemed so real, so vivid. I could feel the anger in my heart as it pulsated through my veins.

Hand to my chest, I closed my eyes and willed it away. That wasn't me. That couldn't have been me. But it looked like me. It even sounded like me. It was just a dream. That's all. A really, really bad dream.

Dragging a hand through my hair, I winced when my hand tangled in a part that had gotten stuck under me. Either I needed a haircut, or I needed to learn how to braid. The image of the maid braiding my hair in the dream made me grimace.

Cutting it was.

Unable to sleep any longer, I threw the covers off and stepped out of bed. My foot stepped on something soft and fuzzy, and a loud yowl followed by a hissing made me jump to the side. Hands over my mouth, I thought I'd stepped on a cat, but the large creature baring its teeth at me was unlike anything I'd seen before.

A mouth full of razor-sharp teeth filled most of its face, its eyes, a deep purple, narrowed as it prowled toward me. While its body was covered in fur, its arms and legs were scaly and green. Its tongue slithered out like a snake and its tail—which had spikes—whipped out behind it.

I held my hands out in front of me, hoping it would ward the little beast off, but it kept coming. I climbed on top of the stool sitting by the vanity, trying to get as far away from it as possible. The height didn't make a difference, its front legs propping up on the stool and its mouth opening wide to take a bite out of me. An ear-piercing scream ripped from my throat as a wet, slimy tongue lapped at my ankles.

My scream turned into a giggle as the creature didn't bite me, but kept licking me. Reaching down, I pushed on its face. "No, no. Down. Stop it. That tickles!"

When I finally got him to stop licking me,
I sat on the stool, petting his head. A moment
later, the door banged open. Gage stood in
the doorway with his sword raised, his eyes
scanning the area for enemies. With his
chest heaving, he asked, "What happened?"

Huffing out a laugh, I stroked the
creature's head. "Uh, nothing. I'm fine."

Gage's dark eyes moved from me to the
creature, and his face could have been
carved from marble at that moment from
what I could see of it. "This?" He gestured a
hand toward the creature, who had begun to
purr under my hands. "This is why you
screamed?"

"Uh, yeah. I thought he was going to bite
me." I turned to the creature and held it by
the sides of its face. "But you're not gonna
bite me, are you? You're just the most
sweetest lizard cat creature I've ever seen.
Yes, you are." The creature waged its tail and
leaned into my grasp.

"She," Gage corrected me, and I looked up
to him and then back down at the creature.

"So, you're a girl." I grinned, scratching
behind her ears. "Of course, you're a girl.
Just look at that silky fur. Oh, yes. Such a
pretty girl."

"I wouldn't go getting attached to that,"
Gage warned, putting his sword up. He was

wearing another one of his tight fitted shirts that showed off all of those muscles and the markings up his arm. My attention drifted from the creature in my hands to the tight leather wrapped around his legs. He made a sound that sounded like a snort crossed with a laugh that had my eyes jolting up to his mostly covered face.

"Why not?" I stared into his dark eyes, scratching once more at the creature's insistence. "She's just a big pussycat."

"Hell beast. She is a hell beast." He glared at the creature, his arms crossing over his large chest. "And she should be with her master."

Brow furrowed, I asked, "Who's her master?"

Just then, in a poof of black and purple, Blake appeared, shirtless and in a frenzy. "There you are!" he cried, reaching toward the hell beast, who jumped from my lap and bounded toward him. She licked his face and chest as he grinned at her. It'd have been really adorable had I not been drooling over his bare chest.

Hidden beneath his robes, I'd never suspected Blake to have such well-defined muscles. He had tattoos of symbols I didn't recognize that glowed and moved where they decorated his skin. The sight was mesmerizing in more ways than one.

As if feeling my eyes on him, Blake's head jerked up. For once, his hair wasn't covering his whole face and his one purple eye met mine, and then it clicked. They were a pair. The hell beast and Blake with their matching purple eyes. I should have noticed it right away.

"You shouldn't be in here, Izzy." Blake turned his eyes back down to the hell beast, rubbing her behind the ears with a soft look on his face. "You could have gotten hurt." It was strange to see such a look on his usually scowling face. However, his words made me want to smack him in the face as usual.

"By who?" I scoffed, standing from my seat. "She was more likely to scare me to death than for me to hurt her."

Shooting me a glare, Blake stood up, one hand still on Izzy's head. "I don't know you. None of us do. For all we know, you're not even a human." He sniffed in my direction. "You could be a spy from—"

"Blake." That one word from Gage made Blake clap his mouth shut. Glaring at me once more, he gathered Izzy up and turned on his heel, stomping out of the room rather than disappearing again.

Sighing, I sat back down on the stool. I felt Gage's eyes on me, and it made me angry. Snapping my head up, I growled, "I don't know anything so stop looking at me like that." When he kept staring at me as if he didn't believe me, I stood and stomped over to him. I shoved a finger at his massive chest. "I'm no more a threat to you than you are to yourself." When he made a face at that, I added, "Okay, fine, maybe not like that, but I'm not going to hurt you. I'm not a spy. I barely know my own name, why would I want to hurt the people who saved me?"

We stared at each other for a long moment, neither one of us wanting to give in and admit defeat. I sighed and shifted my stance, my hands on my hips, and I narrowed my eyes on the large mage, daring him to say something mean.

"I do not doubt your sincerity," Gage announced suddenly. "But there are too many factors to let our guard down for just anyone."

"Oh yeah, I know," I sneered. "The council election, blah, blah."

Gage tensed. "So, you had been listening. And you say you aren't a spy."

I blanched. "That…that was an accident. I was really looking for Zane."

"As you say." Gage narrowed his eyes into slits, not believing a word out of my mouth.

Letting out a frustrated growl, I threw my hands up in the air. "Fine, whatever. Believe what you want. You will anyway." I shoved at his chest, which didn't move an inch. "Now, if you don't mind, I would like to get dressed."

Without a word, Gage left. I slammed the door shut behind him for good measure, though it did nothing to subside the racing of my heart. My frustration at their suspicions had awakened the anger from my dream, and I had to crouch down into a ball to make myself calm down.

Holding my knees to my chest, I rocked back and forth, willing my heart to slow.

It was just a dream. Just a dream. Somehow, I felt that repeating it wasn't going to make it any more untrue.

What the hell was I going to do?

Chapter 10

I'd been with the mages—the men who saved me—for a few days now, and I would like to think we'd sort of settled into a routine.

The last few mornings, I would wake up in my room and get dressed after taking a long, hot shower. I'd finally gotten one of the men to show me how to work the damnable thing which, by the way, has a voice activated panel hidden in the wall to turn it on or off.

"Turn shower on," I told the shiny black screen, which lit up with a soft blue light at my command. The water turned on seconds later, the heat preset to my desired temperature. I was beginning to really enjoy this new world I'd woken up in. They made so many things so much easier.

Climbing into the shower, I let out a long moan of pleasure. So much better than freezing cold bird baths. I could live in the shower. I could probably live in the bath as well, but it was much harder to enjoy with so much hair filling the tub. It was on my agenda today to make sure I find someone to cut the lot of it off for me.

Lathering up the body wash, or so I'd been told it was called, onto a nearby sponge, I scrubbed my skin until it was pink and clean. My hair came next, which was a daunting task that I hoped soon to be done with. Perhaps I'll cut it as short as one of the men's. Then it would take no time at all to wash my hair.

I sighed at the thought, my own daydreams and the water keeping me from hearing the knock on the bathroom door until it opened. A head of bloodred hair peeked into the crack of the bathroom door and I let out a tiny shriek before my foot slipped out from under me and I came tumbling down inside the shower. With glass walls, there was nothing to hold on to on the way down and I ended up in a crumpled heap on the floor.

"Eva!" Zane cried out, hurrying to my side. If I wasn't in so much pain, I'd find the fact that he was trying to help me at the same time as he was trying to keep his eyes on the ceiling a counterintuitive action. "Are you okay?" He cleared his throat several times, his cheeks turning red as he held a towel out to me.

I groaned and pushed myself up. "Yes, just a bit bruised. You startled me."

"My apologies. I knocked, but no one answered. I feared you might have..." Zane shook his head with an embarrassed twitch of his lips. "Never mind. I'm glad you are okay."

Wrapping the towel around myself, I waited until Zane moved before climbing out of the bath/shower. "What did you want?" I paused when I realized I sounded a bit rude and amended it. "I mean, were you looking for me for a reason?"

Zane's eyes shifted over to me with hesitance before he sagged in relief seeing me covered. It'd have made me self-conscious had I not seen him looking at me more often than not with desire in his eyes. They all did. Though, none of them did anything about it. It made me wonder if it was just me or because I was human. I was betting on the latter.

"I thought you would like to see the city today. You haven't been out of this house yet and it would be—"

"Yes!" I shouted, cutting him off and then wincing as I covered my mouth with my hand before quickly adding, "Sorry, I mean, I would love to see the city. I am feeling a bit crazy in here." My eyes widened. "Not that you aren't wonderful company or that your home isn't great, but I was really hoping to find out more about this world or time…" My brows furrowed as I struggled with the right words.

Thankfully, Zane seemed to understand. With a chuckle, Zane nodded. "No offense taken. I would be a bit stir crazy myself after I've been studying for far too long." He pulled his glasses from his face and stared into the lenses from a few inches from his face before putting them back on. "In any case, we'll see about getting you out of the house after some breakfast. Alright?"

I inclined my head with a bright smile. "Sounds wonderful. Thank you."

We stood there for a moment, an awkward silence falling over us. Then Zane shifted his stance, pointing a thumb over his shoulder. "I'll just go and let you get dressed." He cleared his throat. "Uh, yeah."

Then he was out the door faster than a hellhound who was told there was bacon for her. Which I'd recently found out was lightning fast.

Grinning at his back, I went about the long process of drying my hair and then getting dressed. By the time I made it to the kitchen, everyone was there except Gage. I'd noticed that he would pop in and out without explanation and none of them ever asked. It probably had to do with his profession, but I wasn't brave enough to ask.

"There she is." Adam grinned at me before placing my usual mug of coffee with cream in front of me, and then a plate full of steaming food next to it. "We were wondering if you had gotten lost in all that hair of yours."

I flushed as the men around me chuckled. Except for Blake, who frowned harder at his plate. Luke took his usual place next to me at the counter and Zane leaned against the fridge with his own coffee mug in his hands.

Picking up my fork, I began to eat my food under their watchful eyes. One thing I had learned was they loved to watch me eat. Whether it was because they were just curious by nature or because of the small sounds I made each time something touched my tongue I didn't really care enough to figure out. I would feel embarrassed, but I couldn't help it. When you'd gone as long as I had without eating—which I still wasn't sure exactly how long—then you learn to take every meal as your last. Who knew when my next one would be?

"So, Zane was talking about taking you out and about the city today," Adam started conversationally, pulling all of their gazes away from my eating patterns. "What would you like to see?"

I chewed the food in my mouth and lifted a shoulder. "I don't know. Everything."

They snickered at me. Then Luke bumped his shoulder with mine. "Everything is a tall order. But I think we can work something out."

"I also want to get my hair cut," I said quickly before ducking my head.

Silence followed my admission before Zane said, "I don't see how that would be a problem. There are many hair stylists in the area. Luke, yours is fairly open-minded, yes?"

Luke nodded beside me. "Oh, yeah. I'll shoot her a message letting her know we are coming. But are you sure you want to cut it off?" His eyes moved to my long, blonde hair pooling at my feet. "It's so pretty."

Blake snorted. "Of course, she does. Can you imagine having hair that long? What a pain. All the primping. Not to forget how much shampoo you'd have to go through weekly to take care of it. No thank you." He shook his head with disgust.

Taking a page out of their book, I pointed a finger at Blake. "What he said."

Luke shrugged. "Alright, I'll make the arrangements. After we're done eating here we can go."

At his words, I turned back to my food and inhaled it as fast as I could, not caring if I was pretty while doing it. The prospect of getting my hair cut was all the motivation I needed not to dally.

When done, I dropped my fork on my plate with a loud clack and looked up. "Done."

Four pairs of eyes stared at me with a mixture of amusement and horror. I sheepishly lifted my shoulders. "What?"

* * *

"Are you sure you want to do this?" Luke asked again, worry making deep grooves in his forehead.

"Yes." I nodded, a sense of finality in my voice. My fingers digging into the chair's arms did nothing to help me.

"He's right, lovely," the hair stylist, Bea, told me, with a skeptical look on her face. Her fingers stroked through the long strands of my pale blonde hair. "People would kill for your hair."

When Luke had offered to take me to get my hair cut, I never expected him to take me to a woman who had half of her hair cut to the scalp and the rest colored a blueberry blue. I'd gaped for the first five minutes before I remembered myself. I'd snapped my mouth closed and shook her hand, forcing myself not to stare at the glowing ring in her nose or the color changing bar through her eyebrow. Despite my initial surprise, she ended up being quite a nice woman. Opinionated and loud, but nice all the same.

"I'm sure." I nodded again, meeting their eyes in the mirror.

Around us, half a dozen others were sitting in the same position as me. A chair in front of a mirror, a cape around their necks, and a stylist talking their ear off. I didn't remember much about my previous life, but I knew we didn't have anything like this. A special place just to change your hair. The very thought of changing the color of my hair caused palpitations to pulse through my chest. But here, all you had to do was say the word, the stylist flipped their wrist, and BAM you have violet-colored locks.

What was the world coming to?

Sighing, Bea released my hair and moved over to the mirror. "Well, if you're sure, then we have several options that would go great with your face shape." She pressed a swirling blue circle on the edge of the mirror. Suddenly, my reflection changed. My long blonde hair had been cut into a much shorter style, the ends brushing the edge of my jawline. My hand reached up in surprise, grabbing at the new style, but found my hair still long, no hair had been cut.

Giggling, Bea shook her head. "It's not real. Just a simulation. This way you can see how it would look like before we go through with it." She glanced over my head, amusement glittering in her eyes. "She's never been to a stylist, has she?"

Luke cleared his throat and shifted behind me in the mirror. "Uh, she's from outside of the city."

His answer seemed to satisfy Bea, because she went back to the magic mirror. Science, not magic, I reminded myself. Zane had done an excellent job putting the difference into my head. While they had magic at their disposal, they still had to rely heavily on science lest they overuse and abuse magic.

"Magic has a price and shouldn't be used lightly," Zane had told me, cleaning his glasses on his shirt. "You can't just use it to make whatever you want. Believe me, magically made coffee tastes like ash.”

I'd laughed at him, but still didn't get it. What's the point of having magic if you couldn't use it for everything? Probably a good thing I didn't have any then…anymore.

It made the dream I had come to mind. My former self had no problem overusing magic. I would go so far to say she probably abused it often. Shoving those thoughts aside, I turned my attention back to Bea.

“What about this one?” Bea asked, stopping the display of simulations. This one had my hair brushing my shoulders, my bangs sweeping over my forehead to tickle my cheek.

I moved my head this way and that, intrigued by the way the hair moved with me. Glancing up at Luke in the mirror, I asked, “What do you think?”

Crossing his arms over his chest, Luke shrugged. “It's not my hair. I don't have to live with it.”

Bea snorted. “Such a man answer.” To me, she said, “Honey, let me give you some advice. The only reason he would even know you changed your hair is the fact that he's standing right here. Most men aren't that observant.”

"Ain't that the truth!" an older woman in the chair next to me said, lifting a hand in the air. I wasn't much for guessing ages, but I'd have said she was in her mid-sixties based on the wrinkles on her face and the devil-may-care smile on her lip. "My husband and I have been together for forty years, and any time I change my hair, it takes him a month before he notices. If he does at all!" She chuckled and grinned at her stylist, who nodded in agreement.

"Hey, not all men." Luke frowned and then tilted his head to the side. "Okay, so probably Adam and Gage." He ticked them off on his fingers. "And most likely Zane. God knows he doesn't notice anything unless it's in one of his books. But I would have noticed!" he declared, only causing the women in the room to laugh and his face to redden.

Grinning up at him, I reassured him, "I'm sure you would have." To Bea, I declared, "Do it."

"Okay, let's get to it." Bea pressed the spot on the mirror again and grabbed a pair of scissors from the table in front of us.

"What do you need those for? Aren't you going to use magic?" Luke asked, staring at the scissors.

Bea gaped at him. "And lose her first hair cutting experience? I think not. Besides, look at this hair! She could sell the bulk of it for a pretty penny at the potion store. You know how many good spells call for hair as untouched as this?"

Luke pursed his lips together in thought and then placed a hand on my shoulder. "It's up to you. She is right though. Fresh ingredients like yours could set you up for months."

My lips twisted into a thoughtful frown. I didn't really care about money, but then again, I couldn't rely on Luke and the others to take care of me for the rest of my life. A small part of me was saddened at the thought. Did I really think I'd be with them for longer than they could bear? What did they owe me after all?

Nothing, that's what. Not a damn thing.

"Just do it," I said firmly, with a heaviness in my heart that I forced myself to ignore.

Chapter 11

My fingers played with the edges of my new hair. My head felt lighter, that was for sure. Funnily enough, a small part of me, one I didn't know was there, was sad about losing the weight.

In my other hand, I held a bag that had the rest of my hair. Bea had been most gracious to point me in the direction of the shop I could sell it to, which we were heading to right now.

Since it wasn't too far away, Luke decided we should walk rather than taking the car. He had been quiet since we left Bea and the other chattering stylists. Also, he was distant. Unlike at the house, he didn't touch me at random times and made a point to keep his hands to himself, lacing the fingers behind his back.

I felt the eyes on me. It was hard not to notice them. They had been on us since we left the shop. Thankfully, it seemed the horde wasn't that interested in me when I wasn't with the whole group of them...or maybe it was just Adam? He seemed to be the celebrity of the five of them.

Still, they stared.

Even the humans. It was easy to tell the difference between the humans and the mages. It wasn't some magical mark or anything, but the way they held themselves, hunched down, eyes to the ground, except when they were chancing curious and what seemed like jealous looks at me. Also, their clothes were not as regal, I supposed was the word. Plain colors, in simple styles. No golden embellishments or weapons of any kind. It made me look down at my own clothes.

I'd chosen a flowy white blouse with a purple vest. When buttoned it caused my breasts to press up, giving me the illusion of cleavage. A pair of black pants covered my legs, so tight that Luke had done a double take when he'd seen me. On my feet, prune colored boots teased my ankles.

I didn't exactly dress like someone who was supposed to be serving the mages. Not that I was really serving. My last two times trying to cook had ended in black smoke and the men running to the screams of some alarm. I'd since given up cooking for them. They didn't seem too bothered by it though.

"Luke," I started, moving closer to him as another couple passed us. The human trailing after them glanced at me curiously before hurrying after the couple. "Luke," I said again, and a visible tension in his shoulders showed. Getting frustrated, I grabbed his arm and raised my voice. "Lucas."

"Do not touch me," he hissed, sounding more like his brother Blake than his teasing, fun-loving self. Luke jerked his arm from my grasp, his eyes boring into me like he was trying to tell me something before darting around us.

Frowning, I dropped my hand and ducked my head. Had I done something wrong? Chewing on my lip, my mind lost in my thoughts, I stayed quiet until we arrived at our destination.

Luke pushed the glass door open, not waiting for me to follow after him before letting it go. My frown deepened at his lack of manners, catching the door before it hit me in the face. This one-eighty he had done was really starting to get to me. A small part of me was wondering if perhaps he and his brother had made some kind of switch when I wasn't looking.

My irritation briefly disappeared as I gaped at the store around us. There were displays full of bottles that glowed and sparkled. Some had eyeballs in them, while others had teeth or other bits that should never be removed from one's self. I moved closer to one that held what looked like chicken's feet in it. As I stared at it, one claw twitched, making me jump in place, backing away from it quickly. I bumped against a table, knocking a bottle to the ground with a crash.

"Watch it, you wretch!" a glaring, plump woman in pretty mage-like clothes shouted, grabbing me by the wrist. "You better have money to pay for that."

Luke suddenly appeared at my side. With one hard look, the woman released me. "She's with me."

"Of course, Healer. I meant no offense. But who's going to pay for this?" She gestured at the purple substance that had spilled on to the floor, glass shards mixed into it as smoke rose from the pile.

"Put it on my tab." Luke's voice held no room for disagreement, and the woman nodded quickly before hurrying away. When she was gone, Luke turned that glare to me. "Try not to make a mess, or I'll have to take it out of your hide later."

Blanching at his threat, I took a step back from him, my lip quivering. I clamped my hand over my mouth to stop it. I wouldn't cry. I've endured worse.

But why was I having to now? Luke had never spoken to me this way, let alone offer me harm. The very thought of it made me want to run back to my tower and never look back. What was wrong with him?

Turning on his heel, Luke stalked toward the counter. He stopped in front of a thin man who nervously asked him what he could do for him. Luke held up his hand and clicked his fingers several times. I stared at him blankly before he tilted his head toward me, and then I hurried forward.

With an impatient sigh, he pulled the bag of hair from my hand and tossed it on the counter. "I've come to trade."

The man hesitated before taking the bag from Luke. Pulling the tie on it, he reached in and pulled out the long strands of my hair. Glancing down at the hair and then up to me, it was obvious he knew where they had come from. "These are marvelous. Are you sure you don't wish to keep it for your own stores?"

"No," Luke clipped, not allowing for more discussion.

With a curt nod, the man took the bag over to a metal station. He dumped my hair out onto a tray and waited for numbers to show up on a screen. He named off how much he could give for it, an amount that meant nothing to me, but seemed to please Luke.

"Would you like it applied to your tab?" the man asked, moving to the metal box on the counter. It made beeping noises as he pressed the buttons on it.

"No, put it on this," Luke answered, tossing a metal square card on the counter. The man took the card and hurried to a box and placed the card down on a pad of some sort. When he was done, he turned back to Luke and tried to hand it to him, but Luke just stared at him, not putting his hand out. The man then looked at me with a raised brow, holding the card out to me instead.

Not sure what I was supposed to do, but not wanting to get yelled at again, I took the card from him and shoved it in my pocket. Luke spun on his heel and started for the door, leaving me dumbfounded at the counter.

A voice cleared behind me, and the man at the counter nudged his chin toward Luke. My eyes widened as I realized he was telling me to follow him. It seemed that I was now playing the incompetent human to the powerful mage. How did I ever get so lucky?

Doubling my steps, I raced after Luke. My confusion and hurt was quickly morphing into anger, and before I could stop myself, I smacked him on the back. Several witnesses gasped in horror, but I ignored them.

"What the hell was that?" I pushed him in the back once more. Luke spun around and caught my wrist before I could smack him again. Several people, mages and humans alike, had stopped what they were doing to watch the interaction. Fine. Let them look. I wasn't going to be treated this way.

Without looking around at our audience, Luke tightened his grip on my wrist and jerked me toward an alleyway. I struggled against his hold not wanting to get hit like he had promised before.

"Let go of me," I cried out, no longer trying to play nice. I should never have trusted this lot of men. Just because they took me out of my tower didn't mean they were on my side. What was I thinking? I should have taken my chances with the other mage, Master Tuck, no matter how vile he seemed.

As Luke shoved me inside the alleyway, a female mage muttered with a huff, "Serves her right, the filthy, disrespectful human."

Luke dragged me so deep into the alley that the sun barely reached us. Covered by darkness, he pressed me up against the wall, our bodies barely touching each other. Under other circumstances, I'd have blushed and teased Luke for being so forward, but seeing as the light in his eyes was not from attraction but something else, I only felt rage.

"What do you think you are doing?" I shoved at his chest, trying to make him move. "First, you completely ignore me. Then you yell at me. What the ever loving hell is your problem?"

Instead of answering my questions, Luke put his hand over my mouth. He shot a look toward the alley way entrance, where a few nosy mages were still lingering. One glare from Luke made them scatter like ants.

In a spout of childishness, I stuck my tongue out. Luke jerked his hand back and stared at it. "Did you just lick me?"

Crossing my arms over my chest, I sneered, "Maybe I did."

Luke's eyes bore into me intensely, and then suddenly, he broke into a grin. The mage I knew and had come to care for coming to the surface. "I can't believe you did that."

Unable to keep myself from smiling—really, his was infectious—I tightened my arms over my chest. Through gritted teeth, I snapped, "Well, believe it." I winced when it came out less sharp than I intended.

Luke sighed and dragged a hand through his hair. "I'm sorry about all that. When I had decided we should walk, I had forgotten that you were a human. So, when everyone started staring, I realized that if I treated you differently, we were going to draw way too much attention."

The tight furrow of my brow loosened a bit at his explanation. Dropping my arms, I sagged against the wall. "You could have given me a heads up. I thought I'd done something wrong."

"No, no." Luke shook his head, his shaggy hair falling over his face as he leaned one hand on the wall next to me. "You're great. Fantastic really." He reached up and played with the ends of my newly cut hair. "It's my fault. I should have told you."

"Yeah," I murmured, caught up in how close his face had gotten to mine. Trying to break the tension, I dug into my pocket and pulled out the card. "You really should have this. After all, you paid for my hair cut and who knows how much all those clothes you got me cost."

"No way." Luke pressed the hand holding the card back to my chest. "It's yours. Your hair. Your money. Besides, won't it be nice to have something that's yours?" He shifted in place, grinning. "I mean, you must feel a bit like a burden. Though you shouldn't," Luke quickly added. "None of us feel like you are. We love having you there." Ducking his head, his nose brushed mine, his voice lowering. "I mean, I love having you there."

My face heated at his admission and I clutched the card tightly to my chest. "I like being with you too." I tilted my head up slightly to look at him, and our mouths touched.

Shocked, I froze in place, not sure what to do. Luke wasn't as surprised. His hands came up to tangle in my shortened locks as he pressed his mouth firmly against mine. My eyes closed briefly, and I let myself sink into the kiss.

Judging by the overall level of kisses, it was innocent really. Just a press of lips, a brushing really. Luke never tried to deepen it or make it more, a fact I appreciated, but at the same time, it frustrated me. I wanted him to take me into his arms and ravish my mouth like he meant it. On the other hand, I was still so disoriented by the whole experience of not being in the tower, as well as the other morning's dream, that I wasn't sure I was ready for anything more.

When he withdrew, we were both breathless and smiling. A faint blush covered his cheeks as I stared up at him, but the heat in his eyes told me he wasn't so embarrassed by what we had done. Leaning into his embrace, I could have stayed that way forever. Except my stomach had a different idea.

Chuckling at the sound of my stomach growling, Luke wrapped an arm around my waist. "How about we get something to eat?"

I nodded. "Sure, but can we…?" I grimaced at the idea of going back out there and being treated like a lesser being. "Can we just go home and eat?"

Luke's brows furrowed and then his eyes moved to where the alley ended. He frowned at first and then nodded, giving me a reassuring look. "Of course, whatever you want." He wrapped his arms around me tightly, a grin spreading across his lips.

A tingling feeling spread through me and not all from just the feeling of him pressed against me. "What are you doing?"

Laughter in his eyes, Luke hugged me tighter. "Hold on to your socks!" With a whirl of yellow and white, we were gone.

Chapter 12

When Luke and I arrived back at the house, I was feeling a bit better. Then when we walked into the house and everything imploded.

"Izzy! Get back here!" Blake yelled just a moment before Izzy came barging toward me. Izzy tangled between my legs, almost knocking me over, making a pathetic whimpering sound. Right after, Blake appeared in the foyer. His eyes zeroed in on Izzy, and he stared at her until he realized it was me she was hiding behind. His eyes scanned up my legs and over my chest, and then settled on my face. Or more specifically, my hair. "You cut your hair."

"See!" Luke gestured a hand toward Blake. "Someone noticed."

Rolling my eyes at Luke, I flipped my hair over my shoulder before kneeling by Izzy. "What's wrong, girl? Is the grumpy old mage being mean to you?" I rubbed her ears and made kissing sounds at her.

"I am not being mean to her," Blake snapped, stomping over to me. He knelt beside me and held a hand out to Izzy. "Come on, girl, it's not that bad. She didn't mean anything by it."

"She who?" I asked, as a spark of jealousy that had no business being there flared to life.

Blake didn't look at me but at Luke. "Rebecca."

Immediately, Luke tensed beside me. To his brother, with hardness in his voice that I had recently been on the receiving end of and didn't wish it on anyone, he said, "What is she doing here?"

Letting out a disgusted sound, Blake patted Izzy on the head one more time before standing. "She arrived with Master Tuck. Apparently, she's training under him this year."

"Poor bastard." Luke shook his head and then held a finger up. "Actually, I take that back. They deserve each other." The phrase caused Blake and Luke to snicker evilly.

The way Luke talked about this Rebecca person had me frowning hard. He'd never spoken badly of anyone, not to me anyway. To hear him talk about her in such a manner told me more about her than ever meeting her would. Right then, I knew I wouldn't like her.

"Who's Rebecca?" I asked, stroking Izzy to calm my raging nerves. For some reason, I didn't like having another woman in the house, except Izzy. She didn't count. In some way, I had laid claim to the five of them, even if two of the five didn't care for me. Still, an unknown woman in the house, one they didn't talk well about, made me protective.

Blake and Luke shifted uncomfortably, and then Luke sighed. "Rebecca is...a complication."

I stared at him, expecting him to elaborate, but when he didn't, Blake jumped in. "She's Adam's ex." I lifted a brow, not exactly knowing what an 'ex' was. Seeing my confusion, Blake added, "As in ex-girlfriend.

Or I guess you could say more of a lover. Adam doesn't really do girlfriends." He shared a smile with Luke.

"Oh." I couldn't think of anything really to say. I'd never heard of a girlfriend, but the way they were saying it meant Rebecca used to mean something to Adam. The idea of her being in any way cherished by Adam made something tug at my heart. I had no right. I didn't have a claim to them. I barely knew them, and like Gage so blatantly reminded me before, they didn't know me. So then why did I feel like my heart was going to fall out of my butt?

"Hey, don't look so depressed." Luke lifted me to my feet, chucking me under the chin. "No one likes Rebecca, least of all Adam."

Was it weirder that Luke knew I was feeling bad about Rebecca or because he was reassuring me about his friend when he'd not more than half an hour ago kissed me? The reminder that we had been kissing, in a public alleyway no less, made my heart rate pick up and I laced my fingers with Luke's.

Not noticing the way we were smiling at each other knowingly, Blake shook his head. "Come on." He lifted Izzy up into his arms, though it seemed like a struggle. She must be heavier than she looked. "We better get in there before she tries to rip Adam's clothes off with her teeth." The twins visibly shuddered at the exact same time, making me feel slightly better about my position in the household.

Luke led the way down the hallway, but paused when Blake didn't follow us. "Aren't you coming?"

Blake glanced down at Izzy who cowered in his arms. "No, I'm going to put Izzy back in my room. She's had enough abuse from that she-bitch today." His words made Luke snort and shake his head, but he didn't comment.

It was true what people said about animals. They were a great judge of character. This Rebecca woman was looking worse and worse to me. Someone that Izzy, sweet, cuddly Izzy, hated. She had to be evil incarnate.

The words from my dream had slipped in completely unexpectedly. The look on my face—that version of my face—when I thought of them, it made me hug myself tightly. I wasn't that person. It was just a dream.

Chuckling at his brother, Luke wrapped an arm around my waist and ushered me down the hallway. "Come on, lovely. We better get in there. Blake wasn't kidding about her taking Adam's clothes off. She did it during the Summer Solstice festival. He ended up chaining her to the shower head just to keep her off him."

I couldn't help the giggle that came out of me at the visual. However, that laughter and the vision promptly died when we stepped into an office. Master Tuck, Adam, Zane, and a woman I didn't know filled the room. My eyes immediately found the strange woman. This must be Rebecca.

Long, chestnut colored hair fell in waves down the only woman in the office's back. Full, pouty lips and heavily lidded eyes filled a perfectly symmetrical face. She leaned up against Adam and his desk, her breasts practically falling out of the top of her skintight dress, which she might as well not even be wearing with how short it was.

I hated her already, and I hadn't even talked to her. I wasn't the type to judge someone by what they decided to wear—or at least I hoped I wasn't—but everything about this woman screamed she-bitch just like Blake said. The only saving grace was the grimace on Adam's face. The moment his eyes found me, they lit up.

"Eva, you cut your hair!" He smiled brightly, causing Rebecca to scowl at his attention on me.

My hand reached up to touch my head, forgetting I had done just that. With a shy smile, I said softly, "Yeah, I did."

"It looks good." Adam nodded, an appreciative look spreading across his face.

I could feel the pure hate coming in my direction and I risked a look in the gorgeous woman's direction. A look of death zeroed in on me from Rebecca as she sized me up. When she was done looking me over, Rebecca lifted her nose in the air with a huff in what I assumed meant I wasn't worthy of whatever she was thinking.

However, the combination of the way Adam was looking at me and the death glare pinning me to the spot made the tension in the room palpable. I didn't pay much attention to the rest of the occupants until Zane cleared his throat, pulling my gaze to him.

"I have to agree with Adam." Zane gestured his crossed hands toward me, leaning against the bookshelf on the other side of the room. "Your hairstyle is quite fetching." He adjusted his glasses as I dipped my head demurely.

Zane was dressed far more formally than normal. His robe pulled closed over his shirt, not allowing the tattoo that sat on his chest to peek out. His hair was newly washed and braided, hanging over one shoulder. Had I not been living with him the last few days, I wouldn't have noticed the way his shoulders bunched up as if he were completely unable to relax in Master Tuck and Rebecca's presence.

"Thank you." I pulled my bottom lip in between my teeth, smiling despite myself. Zane's lips tipped up even further, making me happy to have relieved at least a little bit of his tension.

"So, she cut her hair, big deal. She's still a filthy human. Why is she even here?" Rebecca snorted, crossing her arms over her chest, which caused her breasts to push up even higher. If it bothered her that her chest was just moments from popping out of her dress, she didn't show it.

"Because I want her here," Adam clipped out, not even tempted by her tantalizing chest. Rebecca tensed slightly, but then shrugged as if she were used to his moods.

Any other human in my situation probably would have been offended. Still, since I hardly remembered my name, let alone what should make me mad, I simply stared at her. This only seemed to irritate her more as she shoved off the desk and sashayed over to me.

"Look at her. She doesn't even have enough brain cells in her head to know when she's being insulted." Rebecca reached out as if to touch me, but Adam caught her hand.

"Don't."

That one simple word from him caused her to frown and drop her hand. Not even close to being mollified, she moved over to Master Tuck and sat on the arm of the chair he sat in. Crossing one leg over the other, she placed a hand on the back of the chair and leaned into Master Tuck. The older mage didn't seem to mind one way or the other, but did well not to stare at her chest so close to his face. Master Tuck's eyes were all for me.

While he might not want the others to know how interested in me he was, Tuck wasn't hiding his eagerness in his gaze. What did that look mean? What did he want with me? I wouldn't be used against Adam like he and Gage had talked about in the library. These men had taken care of me when from what I could see, no one else in the world would have.

Luke squeezed my hand, and I glanced up at him. The reassuring look on his face was probably meant to tell me that while Rebecca might find me a filthy human, he didn't. If our kiss earlier hadn't been proof enough of his allegiance, the way he stood beside me now did.

"Rebecca, dear. Do not lower yourself to this human's level," Master Tuck warned, shaking his head disapprovingly. He shifted in the chair he sat in, his robe even more elaborate than the first one I saw him in. His gaze turned to me, but he didn't stand from his chair. "I see you have acclimated yourself to your situation. I hope Master Adam and the others are treating you well?"

I glanced at Adam with a small smile and said, "Yes, my experience has been most pleasant."

Master Tuck seemed pleased by my answer and turned in his seat more to face me. "And have you recovered any of your memories?"

I paused and glanced at the others, not sure what I should tell and what I shouldn't. When Adam gave me a short nod, I turned my attention back to Master Tuck. I shook my head, my shorter locks now bouncing off my face, causing them to tickle my skin. "No, not really. I get bits and pieces, but not enough to put a whole memory together."

I didn't mention the dream I had. I hardly thought the bloodthirsty mage-hating version of me was something that would endear me to anyone in that room, whether or not they already liked me. Plus, I was still holding on to the hope that it was just a bad dream and not really me. Maybe my subconscious was trying to play tricks on me?

Adam saved me from more questioning as he turned back toward the mage. "Not that we aren't delighted about your visit, Master Tuck, but is there a reason for it?"

If the older mage was offended by Adam's question, he hid it well. I really couldn't even tell what he or the rest of the room were thinking. Well, besides Rebecca, who looked like she wanted to kill me even more than she did before. I should work on my face more. I was far too easily read.

"Ah, yes. Pardon me for the intrusion." Master Tuck cleared his throat and then turned to Zane. "I heard you have been helping our human mystery research what could have happened to her." Zane inclined his head, but didn't answer. "I was wondering how that was going? You know, I am partial to a good intrigue."

Zane cleared his throat and shifted against the bookshelf as if he didn't really want to talk about it with him, but didn't have a choice. "Unfortunately, our findings have been slim. We don't have much to go on really. A tower cloaked by magic with sigils of an unknown origin." Zane met my eyes with a curious intensity. "Eva seems to be

156

quite the academic anomaly. I doubt we will find anything of use here."

That seemed to be just what Master Tuck was looking for. He patted his hand on the arm of the chair, excitement on his face. "Well, then it's settled." He stood from his seat and started toward me. "The human will come back with me to Headquarters where she will have a better chance at finding out her origins."

Master Tuck reached out toward me, and I backed away without meaning to, my back pressing up against Luke's chest. My pulse raced as my eyes widened, I might not have found out much from my stay here, but I certainly didn't want to go with Master Tuck and the she-bitch, I mean Rebecca. Can't let myself slip up on that out loud. Though, it seems the men had no qualms with calling her it to her face.

Just when I thought Master Tuck might actually get his hands on me, Luke's hand settled on my shoulder, and my gaze shot up to his.

"Eva." Luke's voice was hard, like it had been when we were on the streets. "Her name is Eva, and she's not going anywhere."

157

Chapter 13

The expression on Master Tuck's face at Luke's veiled threat was comical. His face paled, and his eyes widened, his lips flapping open and closed like a fish.

"Well, I..." Master Tuck stumbled over his words, clearly not expecting to be fought on this. He turned to Adam, his brows lifted. "Master Adam, certainly you see that Eva," He shot a glance at Luke and then back to Adam, "would be in better care at Headquarters where the whole of the mage council could help her."

I hoped that Adam saw through Master Tuck's words. The insistence of his need for me to go with him, along with the interest in his eyes when he looked at me when he thought the others weren't looking, told me that he didn't plan to just help me find out who I was. He had plans for me. Plans that most certainly wouldn't be good for me or my rescuers.

Adam stared at Master Tuck for a long, hard minute before his eyes slid over to me. "Do you wish to go with him, Eva?" The way he asked it seemed clinical, as if I meant nothing to him, but his eyes said something entirely different. He didn't want me to go.

Swallowing thickly, I shook my head once more. "No, I want to stay here."

Master Tuck scoffed, "What does she know? She doesn't even remember who she is, let alone know what is right for her." The sneer on his lips broke his 'I'm your friend' facade. I was undoubtedly making the right decision in not going with him.

Luke's hand tightened on my shoulder as if making certain I didn't get away. "She knows well enough where she feels safest and that, right now, is here."

"Exactly." Zane stepped in, pushing his glasses further up his face as he brought a more intellectual point of view to the table. "Isn't it better to keep her environment consistent to cultivate her memories?"

"Well, I suppose," Master Tuck answered, seeming less annoyed and more confused. No doubt trying to figure out how this had gotten all turned around on him. Rebecca didn't seem happy about any of it either. The longer they sat there debating my existence, the more annoyed she became.

Adam seemed to catch on to Zane's thought process rather quickly. "I think that it is best to keep Eva here. Perhaps when she has remembered more or has become more accustomed to our ways, we can see about moving her to Headquarters." He raised a brow at Master Tuck as if daring him to argue with him.

Master Tuck pressed his lips together until they were almost nonexistent before letting out a defeated sigh. "Very well. It was only a suggestion," he said, trying to downplay his desire to have me in his clutches. Then, as if he hadn't been defeated, his gaze seemed to harden as he stared Adam down. "Nevertheless, if she is going to stay with you, you must teach her about her place in this world. She will attract the wrong kind of attention if she is not aware of her station." The slight up tilt of his lips was echoed by Rebecca who seemed only too pleased for me to be put in my place.

My back stiffened at the thought of them putting me in my place. Echoes of the way Luke had treated me while we were in public came to mind, and I hoped that there wouldn't be a repeat performance.

"We will make sure she does," Adam assured him, and then swept his arm toward the office door. "If you do not mind, I have other matters to attend to."

"Of course, of course." Master Tuck nodded and tugged his robe closer to himself. "Come, Rebecca. We have other appointments." He started for the door, but then paused at the entryway and turned back to me. "If you change your mind, please let me know. I am only here to help." He twisted his wrist and a glowing blue and black card much smaller than the one I'd been given from Luke appeared between his two fingers. He held it out to me and I hesitated but then took it, not wanting to be rude.

Not knowing what else to say, I simply nodded. I had no intention of calling him or whatever else he wanted me to do. In fact, if

I never saw him again I would be one happy woman.

Taking my nod as an answer, Master Tuck left the room, unfortunately not waiting for Rebecca to follow. She lingered behind, her eyes no longer acknowledging me. Those pretty eyes were solely on Adam.

Without permission or care, she pressed the length of her body against him, her hands coming up to cup his face. "Don't forget what I said, lover. I'm more than willing to work this out." Her eyes skittered over to me slightly before narrowing on Adam. "I'd even be happy to train your human for you if it would get me back into your good graces."

This apparently was the wrong thing to say, because Adam grabbed her wrists and threw them from his face. His eyes were colder than ice. "You are far from my good graces, and insulting Eva is not one of the ways to get back into them. If you were smart, you would give up the idea of us, because it will never happen...ever again."

Rebecca seemed a bit hurt by his words but soon straightened her back, turning her anger toward me. "Don't get any ideas into that filthy head of yours. He's mine, and you don't deserve to even breathe the same air as him."

The others tensed at her words. Adam let out a warning growl, but before he could chastise her once more, she stalked out of the room, her hips swaying aggressively from side to side.

I gaped at her, not sure what I'd done to cause her to hate me so. If I had been the Eva in my dream, it would have been different. It was easy to see how anyone could hate her, but me? I hadn't done anything. I could count on one hand the number of words I have spoken to her and still have five of them left!

Thankfully, once Rebecca was gone, the room seemed to sag. Zane played with the cross around his neck, a pensive expression on his face. A less intense version of it settled on Adam's face, but none the less worrying. Luke was the only one who didn't seem too caught up on Master Tuck's visit.

Luke's hand dropped from my shoulder, and he gave me a small smile before saying, "I'm going to go let Blake know that the she-bitch is gone."

Zane shot him a disapproving look, which Luke promptly ignored. Leaning down to my eye level, Luke brushed his lips against my cheek. I blushed and darted a look at Zane and Adam, who only seemed amused.

"I better get going as well." Zane moved from the bookshelf and toward the door. "If we don't find something soon, I have no doubt Master Tuck will be on our doorstep again, and I'm not sure we can keep him from taking you a second time around."

"Just let him try," Luke growled, a possessive glint in his eyes. I placed a hand on his arm, urging him to calm down. I didn't want any of them to get in trouble because of me, despite what my dream-Eva thought of mages.

"Calm down, Lucas," Adam sighed, dragging a hand through his blond hair. "No one is taking anyone. Go tell your brother before he and Izzy have a conniption." Turning to Zane, he said, "Do whatever you need to do to find out why Eva was in that tower and do it fast. Dig into the locked archives if you have to." Zane stared at Adam for a moment and then gave a jerk of his head.

When Zane and Luke had left the room, I stood in the doorway of Adam's office, not sure what I should do. Did I leave? Or stay? Whatever I should have done, Adam decided for me.

"I wanted to talk to you alone." Adam moved over to his desk, but didn't go behind it. Instead, propping his hip up against the edge. He gestured toward the chair Master Tuck had vacated. I hesitated for just a moment before taking a seat.

My hands folded in my lap, I glanced up at him beneath my lashes. I didn't know why, but my heartbeat sped up from just being alone and under his singular intense gaze. "W-What did you want to talk to me about?" I stuttered out, my mouth going dry.

Adam stared at me for a moment, not saying anything, and then he let out a heavy breath. "Gage told me you overheard us in the library."

I blanched and hurried to say, "I wasn't spying on you. I swear. Like I told Gage, I was really looking for Zane." My fingers twisted around themselves as I tried to explain what happened.

"And I believe you." Adam inclined his head, his lips tilting up slightly. "Actually, I wanted to apologize."

"Apologize?" My brows and pitch raised with my surprise. "For what?"

Adam shifted and gave a short laugh. "See, if you were any other woman, human or not, you would have required, no, demanded an apology." He moved away from the desk and came closer to me, his hands on either side of my chair, my face heating at his closeness. "I can't tell what intrigues me more. The mystery surrounding you that none of us can unravel or that I can make you blush with my mere presence." Adam's voice lowered, his hand coming up to brush my hair away from my cheek. "In any case, you have charmed more than just young Lucas."

At the mention of Luke, my face flushed even more. Did he know that we had kissed? Did it bother him? I was drawn to him the same way I was drawn to Luke and Zane. And if I was honest with myself, even to Gage and Blake who still hated me.

His eyes searched my face and then dipped to my lips. His thumb stroked my lower lip, causing my mouth to part. My heart pounded like a thunderous drum as he moved closer. He was going to kiss me. His breath was hot on my mouth. The desire to taste him suddenly so strong. I should push him away. I should tell him no.

It hadn't been that long since Luke kissed me. While we hadn't made any proclamations of love to each other, a part of me didn't think it would be right to kiss Adam after kissing his friend. Nevertheless, my eyes fluttered closed and my mouth tilted up to meet his kiss...a kiss that never came.

When my eyes opened, I found Adam on the other side of the room, his back to me. My mouth snapped shut, and I swallowed the building saliva, licking my dry lips. I waited for him to say something about what almost happened, but he didn't. Instead, he pulled a book from his shelf and tossed it on the desk, still not looking at me.

Adam's hand twisted, and his usual book appeared in his palm, he leaned against the back side of his desk, his face still away from me. For a moment, I thought he was dismissing me, but then he said without looking up from his book, "You should take a look at that. It might help in figuring out who you are." The strain in his voice was the only sign that he even acknowledged what had just happened.

Standing, I took the book from the table. Palming it in my hands, I stared at his back, wishing he would look at me and not his book. Apparently, this wasn't a wish-granting day, because he never so much as flinched. Sighing, I took my book and left. I had plenty of other things to worry about than almost kisses with my host, even if it would plague me for the rest of the day.

Chapter 14

I didn't even look at Adam's book as I lugged it around the house with me. I went to the kitchen, not really knowing where I was going until I arrived. Thankfully, it was empty for once, an odd occurrence in a house full of men.

Sitting my book on the center counter, I opened the refrigerator. Cool air brushed my heated skin, and for a moment I just stood in the doorway. Breathe in, breathe out. You're fine. Everything is fine.

Who was I kidding? Everything was decidedly *not* fine.

I was a human years, maybe centuries, out of my time, stuck in a world where humans were a subservient species, something I appeared to be. The five men who were keeping me safe, well, half of them, thought they should put me back where they had found me while the other half...I wasn't quite sure how any of them felt, but I knew it was messing with my head.

The biggest worry was the woman I saw in my dream. Dream-Eva. She had to be part of this. I was still in denial that the woman in my dream was me, but if I were going to find any kind of clue as to where to look, it would be her.

"You know, you really shouldn't leave the refrigerator open, you'll let all the cold air out."

I jumped at the voice, spinning around to see Blake at the center counter. His brows rose, and his eyes went to the refrigerator. I shuffled around to close it. Turning back to him, I saw him flipping through the book Adam gave me.

"So, fairy tales, huh?" Blake clucked his tongue. "I never thought you were the type." His one golden eye flicked up to me, a smirk tugging at his lips. "Then again, we did find you in a tower." For a moment, his eyes skimmed over my form, and for the briefest second, I thought I saw desire there. As quick as it came, his usual sneer covered it.

Moving over to him but being careful not to touch him, I stopped at his elbow. Wouldn't want him to throw a fit and leave. Touchy Blake was. "This is a book of fairy tales?" I glanced over his arm and then after a moment of staring down at the words and pictures, I asked, "What's a fairy tale?"

Blake snorted and shot me a look. "You're seriously asking me that?" When I didn't make to change my question, he sighed and tapped the book. "These are fairy tales. *Cinderella. The Little Mermaid. Rapunzel.*" My brow rose at the last one, but I didn't say anything. "A bunch of folklore and myths that were twisted into happily ever afters when they really ended in blood and horrors."

They didn't sound like anything I wanted to read, but the memory of Dream-Eva and her rage sounded like it would be more up her alley.

"Okay?" I drew out the word, more confused about why Adam would give me the book than before. "What does any of those have to do with me? I'm not even this

Rapunzel person you called me before. I'm just...me. Eva. No last name. Apparently, a human stuck in a world I don't belong in."

With a sigh, Blake spun the book around to face me. He pushed it toward me, his finger tapping the cream-colored paper.

I stared down at the page where a similar tower to my prison was painted. In the window of the tower stood a woman, her long yellow hair falling from the window to the ground below where a lone man waited. The woman looked nothing like me and anyone with hair that long wouldn't even be able to move, but still, something played in my mind.

Like a voice whispering in my ear, it taunted me. "Rapunzel, Rapunzel, let down your hair." I shook my head to clear the voice and the blurred woman's face that came with it.

"Anything?" Blake leaned on his elbows toward me, searching my face for some kind of recognition.

Pushing the book away, my heart jumping against my chest, I stepped back. "No. Nothing."

I moved over to the other counter where the machine that I knew made coffee sat. I stared at the strange contraption, the different buttons confusing me. I pushed one, and hot liquid came pouring out. Yelping, I hopped backward and into a firm surface, namely Blake.

"Jeez," he cursed, shoving me out of the way. He pushed a button, stopping the machine and then glared at me. "Why don't you ask next time instead of making a mess?"

"Sorry," I muttered, my eyes darting downward. I reached for a washcloth on the counter and began to clean up the mess.

"What are you doing?"

I stopped mopping up the cooling liquid and stared up at him. "What does it look like I'm doing?" I gestured to the ground with the wet cloth. "Isn't this part of my 'position?'"

Blake rolled his eyes. He put his fingers to his mouth and whistled. The ground shook slightly, and a moment later Izzy came pounding into the kitchen. She stopped briefly to lick across the side of my face, making me giggle and grimace, before she turned her attention to the puddle on the floor.

As she lapped it up, I glanced at Blake. "Should she be drinking that? I mean, won't it make her sick?"

"Pfft, she's a hell beast, she'll be fine." He put his hands on his hips, his brow furrowing. "Actually, maybe I shouldn't let her drink caffeine. I mean, she's already hyper enough." Blake snapped his fingers at Izzy. "That's enough, Izzy."

But the hell beast didn't pay him any mind and kept licking up the coffee. Blake nudged her in the side, but still, she ignored him. Growling, the air in the room began to thicken, and a slight breeze came out of nowhere, brushing Blake's hair away from his face and bringing his scarred eye into view.

"Eliza," he commanded, his voice full of power. "That is enough!"

Izzy shuddered as the power rippled through her, and she bowed her head, whimpering. Even though she had stopped, Blake still pushed his power down on her, bringing her down to her chest.

"Stop it!" I shouted, shoving a hand at him as I knelt by the cowering beast. "You're hurting her."

"I'm not hurting her," Blake snapped, the power still thick in his voice. "She disobeyed, I am reasserting my dominance over her. What do you know about it?"

"Well, you don't have to be such a dick head about it." I glowered up at him, holding Izzy close to me.

Blake stared at me, his purple eye flashing menacingly, until all of a sudden, he started laughing. The power around us settled, and Blake shook his head. "Where did you hear that phrase?"

Frowning, I stared up at him. "Uh, your brother."

Still chuckling, Blake rubbed a hand over his face. "Of course you did." Sighing, he reached up into the cupboard and pulled down a cup. He put it underneath the machine and pushed the same button I did, except this time the hot liquid went into the cup and not all over the floor. "Here." He handed me the cup when it was done.

Turning on his heels, he said over his shoulder, "Try not to make a mess."

Staring pensively down at my cup of coffee, I tried to figure out what he meant by that. Don't make a mess in the kitchen or in general? It was hard to tell since I could do either pretty easily.

Giving Izzy another pat, I stood and started for the door. My eyes caught sight of the book of fairy tales and I paused. For some reason unbeknown to me, I grabbed the book. Who knew? It might give me some kind of clue to who I was and what I was doing here.

I carried my coffee and the book to the library with Izzy close on my heels. No one was in the library yet, blessedly. Zane must be looking for answers somewhere else.

Sitting my book and cup on the nearest table, I sat down. I took a tentative sip of my coffee and grimaced. Glancing down at the dark liquid, I suddenly remembered I forgot the flavored cream Zane had given me before.

Sighing at the waste of a cup, I flipped open the book and scanned the pages of the story of Rapunzel. An evil witch trapped a young girl in a tower. Over the years, her golden hair grew so long that the evil witch would call up to her, "Rapunzel, Rapunzel let down your hair, so that I may climb thy golden stair." Rapunzel would hang her hair out the window so the witch could climb it. The witch was the only tie to the outside world.

I tugged on my own pale locks and grimaced. Youch. Long hair or not, that had to hurt. I turned my gaze back to the story.

Eventually, a prince heard Rapunzel singing and came to the tower. They fell in love and planned to run away together, except the evil witch finds out and cut off Rapunzel's hair.

The story does end happily with the prince and Rapunzel getting together in the end. Still, it left a bitter taste in my mouth. Or maybe that was the coffee I'd accidentally sipped again.

"Is that Blake's doing?" Zane asked, gesturing toward my cup as he came around the table. I hadn't even heard him come in.

I played with the edge of my cup and grimaced again. "Yeah. I kind of made a mess in the kitchen, and then when Blake got it for me, I forgot about the stuff you put in it before."

Zane smiled and placed his hand over my cup. My hand twitched when his palm brushed my fingers. When he removed his hand, the black color had changed to a creamy brown. I picked up my cup again, taking a deep breath in of the sweet-scented coffee.

Taking a sip, I sighed. That was the good stuff.

"Better?" Zane asked with a raised brow, amusement in his eyes.

Taking another drink, I hummed. "Yes, very much. Thank you."

Sitting down in the chair next to me, Zane tapped the book in front of me. "What are you reading?"

Sighing, I snapped it shut. "A book of fairy tales Adam gave me."

Brow furrowed, Zane pushed his glasses back up the bridge of his nose. "Why would he do that?"

I shrugged. "I don't know. Maybe because you found me in a tower and the whole Rapunzel story? Anyway, I didn't find anything useful in it. Nothing that triggered any memories or anything anyway." I glared at the book as if it should have all the answers and had betrayed me by not telling me everything.

"Well, I've been thinking a lot about that." Zane grabbed a bag he had sat on the ground and put it on the table. Pulling out books from it, he searched through them until he found the one he wanted. "You see, I think we are going about this all wrong. Instead of trying to figure out who you are and why you were in that tower, we should be trying to figure out when you are—" He paused for a moment and then shook his head. "I mean—"

I placed my hand on his, stopping him from going further. "I understand. So, how do you propose we do that?" I ignored the tingling feeling that came from touching his hand and glanced down at the book in front of us.

Zane didn't ignore our touching hands as much as I did, his eyes lingering on our joined hands. After a moment, he licked his lips and cleared his throat before dragging his hand out from under mine. He flipped the book open, landing on the cover page.

"A Case of the Ages: From Early Man to the Age of the Mages," I read aloud and then frowned. "So, you want me to read all of our histories?"

"No, no." Zane shook his head and smiled. "I think we can narrow down what time frame you are from by what little you do remember." He pulled his glasses off and turned to look at me. "I mean, you remember how to talk. How to eat. Take a bath. All those little things you didn't need help remembering, right?"

"Right."

"Right, so we start there." He scraped his chair closer to mine. "You didn't know what coffee was or the refrigerator, but you recognized the stove, right?"

"Yes, though yours is strange. I don't remember it looking quite like that."

"Okay, so what does it look like?" Zane urged me on, a sort of excitement in his voice.

Bemused by his energy, I closed my eyes and thought of what a stove looked like. As an image came to mind, I said it out loud. "Stone. Sometimes made of brick or clay with an open fire. When I was little, we didn't have anything that fancy, only a pot that hung over the fireplace."

"Excellent!"

My eyes popped open at Zane's shout, and I watched with curiosity as he flipped through the book quickly. "What? Did it help?" Hope welled in my chest, but I shoved it down, not willing to let myself get too excited.

"Yes, of course it did." He stopped on a page and pointed at the book. "Now, this isn't precise, and it's just an educated guess, but I think you were locked in that tower during the Middle Ages. Maybe even around the time the Necronite meteor fell to earth."

He seemed very worked up about the whole thing, and I didn't have the heart to interrupt him, even though I was bursting with questions. "I mean, I did a bit of research on my own since you arrived. Those sigils were too old for me to know right off the bat, but I was able to find them in some of the early mage journals."

He dug into his bag once more, pulling out a tightly bound book about ready to fall apart. "Those sigils weren't just meant to keep you alive, or they would have just put you to sleep. Sleeping curses were a big thing back then," he explained to me as he flipped through the book. "I could surmise they meant to keep you alive but to do it without a sleeping curse, which means they wanted you alive and aware. If the glamour on the tower hadn't broken or fallen, whichever it was—I'm still not sure—you could have been there..." He trailed off as if not wanting to tell me.

"Zane," I urged him to continue. My heart was already going at a rampant pace. The thought that someone had the option to put me to sleep but instead choose to make me suffer my own company made me worry that I might indeed have done something bad. Something like Dream-Eva had been thinking. Witch. Demon. Evil. The harsh whispers burned my mind and I closed my eyes for a second to push them back.

Zane took my hand in his, making me open my eyes once more. He peered into my eyes, the pity there making my heart hurt. "Well, in theory, it would have held you forever."

"Forever?" I gasped, my hand tightening around Zane's. Forever in that tower. Well, before they found me, I wouldn't have even thought about how long I would be in that tower. Hell, I hadn't even been in my right mind. Still wasn't. But the idea of forever just astounded me far more than anything I'd seen or heard so far.

I must have been really evil for someone to hate me enough to make me suffer for that long.

Chapter 15

"Forever isn't long enough in my opinion."

My head jerked up at Zane's words, his hand stroked mine in long, languid strokes. I swallowed and stared at Zane. He looked the same. Nothing was different save his eyes, but I knew at once that I wasn't talking to Zane anymore. It was the demon.

I tried to jerk my hand out of his grasp, but he held tight, lacing his fingers with mine. With his other hand, the demon removed Zane's glasses and set them on the table. He ripped the hair tie from his hair and shook his head, causing Zane's red locks to fall over his face, a wicked grin creeping up his face.

"That's better. That mage always did hold himself too tightly together." The demon shook Zane's body as if trying to find the right fit. I forced myself not to panic as he took his sweet time, my eyes searching around for some way to get away from him. Gage wasn't here this time to save me, and I was clearly out of my depth.

When the demon seemed to be satisfied with Zane's body, he shifted closer to me. "You must have been one nasty piece of work, my lovely," he purred, his tongue peeking out to lick his lips in a vulgar manner.

"You shouldn't be here," I told him harshly, pulling on my hand again but to no avail. "You better go before someone comes to check on us."

"I just want to talk," the demon purred as he tried to reassure me, but the gleam in his eye told me he had more than talking on his mind. If it had been Zane, I might have been more receiving of his salacious looks, but the demon reeked of evil, so much so that my skin prickled at his very touch.

"Zane's going to be upset," I said, attempting once more to get the demon to go away.

The demon threw Zane's head back and laughed, a dark laugh that caused a shiver down my spine. "The cleric is all too excited about you, I doubt he will emerge any time soon. He's just as intrigued by you as I am." He leaned forward until his nose pressed to the side of my neck. I stayed as still as possible as he took a big whiff. "Ah, the naughty thoughts going through his mind. You should see what he thinks of doing to you. The way he craves your body. Your touch. Truly worth eternal damnation." He withdrew from me, smirking. "Just like you."

"What about me?" I should scream at the top of my lungs, fight him, or try and get Zane back, but his words made me pause.

"Oh, my lovely." He lifted our joined hands to his mouth, his tongue snaking out to lap at my hand. "You know what you are. You feel it in your blood. Just like I can taste it on your skin."

My nose scrunched up in a grimace at the wet feeling of his tongue on my hand. His words hardly affected me compared to the urgent need to wash myself clean of his touch. A part of me wondered if I would have been so disgusted had it actually been Zane doing these things to me. Not that he would. Zane didn't seem the type to make an advance on his own.

Shaking my head, I tried to process the words the demon was spouting out. "No, no. I'm not like you. I'm not evil."

Even as I said the words, images of the woman in my dream appeared without permission. It was clear that woman was not someone who had the love of the people. If that woman was me—and I wasn't a hundred percent on board with it—then what the demon was saying might just be true.

No, I couldn't let him get to me. That was what he wanted. When the demon simply grinned at me, I shoved my chair back, standing as I ripped my hand from his grasp. This time he let me, all the while laughing.

"Stop. Just stop it," I snarled, my hands balling into fists as I glared down at him. "You don't know me. Hell, I don't even know me. So how could you know what I do or do not deserve?" I gnashed my teeth at him, trying to be as intimidating as possible, but the demon wasn't fooled.

"Deny it all you like, but you know you deserved to be in that tower. That you were never supposed to be found." He stood from his seat and stalked toward me. My feet stumbled backward as he prowled after me. I kept my eyes on him, my head shaking back and forth, but he kept coming.

"You don't know what you're talking about," I said, tears burning my eyes. It couldn't be true. It can't be.

"Oh, lovely Eva," the demon purred, and rolled his neck from side to side as if really getting ready to chase me. "If I know one thing...it's evil, and you are undoubtedly pure evil."

"No, I'm not." I threw a book at him, but he dodged it with a laugh.

"Don't distress. You should embrace it. Nothing in this world feels better than being bad." He locked his eyes on mine with a full toothed grin as he taunted, "You know you want to."

"No, I don't," I declared firmly, before I darted around a bookshelf, hoping to put some distance between us.

Peeking through the books on the shelf, I saw the demon staring back at me. Letting out a squeal, I barely ducked before a shelf full of books came tumbling out on top of me. My hands above my head, I curled into myself to avoid as much damage as possible.

While I was distracted by falling books, the demon wearing Zane's face took that moment to sneak up on me. His hands wrapped around my waist and pulled me flush against his chest. Laughing as I struggled, the demon moved his hands beneath the edge of my shirt, his fingers moving closer to my breasts. Not wanting his hands on me for one more moment, I reached up and grabbed a handful of his hair, ripping at it viciously.

"You bitch!"

The demon's hands released me as he fought to get his hair away from me, but the moment he let go, I twisted around. My nails clawed into the side of his face, causing him to shout. His palm clutched his now bleeding face, and the demon was distracted enough for me to dart around the bookshelf and toward the door.

Before I could reach the library door and my only hope, a hand twisted in my hair, jerking me back. I knew I should have gone for the bob cut!

The hand shoved at my back, throwing me into a nearby table. Pain shot through my back as I landed, and I cried out. Before I could search for an escape route, he was on me. His arms caged me in. His face hovered over mine. Three scratches decorated the side of his face. They were already beginning to heal, only a small amount of blood even showed that I had hurt him.

My chest rose and fell rapidly as I tried to catch my breath, and at the same time not evoke the demon's wrath further. If it weren't for the look in the monster's eyes, I could almost pretend it was Zane pressed up against me. That look was a dangerous one, the kind that told me he'd just as much take me to bed as he would kill me.

"You don't want to do this," I implored him, though I knew it was useless. My running had only caused him to be even more interested in me. Like a wolf to the lamb.

"Of course I do," the demon growled, flashing a feral grin. His fingers trailed along the outside of my thighs and then, all of a sudden, lifted me up on the table.

I gasped, my hands coming up to Zane's chest. One hand came up and gripped my chin, forcing my face toward him. "But what will I do to you? What would make the cleric suffer the most?" His mouth passed over mine, nipping at my lips.

I swallowed hard, my mind racing for some way out of this. Though I loathed it, my mind immediately thought someone would come for me. Someone would find me. Stop him like before. Right?

"I could kill you right here." His grip tightened until I winced. "Make it slow and painful, maybe even bring the cleric to the surface just long enough for him to watch you die." I whimpered slightly, and to my dismay, the sound only made him grin more. "Or..." his eyes trailed down my face and settled on my exposed cleavage. "I could think of something else that would make the cleric suffer even more."

"W-What's that?" I stuttered and then cleared my throat. I wouldn't let him see my fear anymore. It only seemed to excite him more. Maybe if I kept him talking, bided my time, Zane would come back.

His lips curved up. "I could take you right here. He wants me to, you know? He would love nothing more than to be deep inside of you and what better way to torture him than to give him what he wants and then let him live in the aftermath of what he's done." He ground his hips into mine, and my body jolted in response.

I wouldn't let myself be a victim. I wouldn't be helpless, not again.

My blood raced through my veins as my hand found the skin beneath his shirt. I could play along until he was at his most vulnerable. But then what? I didn't have a weapon. How would I get away? I didn't want to hurt him because that would hurt Zane. The fact that I had already hurt the cleric pained me. But what else could I possibly do?

As if waiting for my most desperate moment, something rose up inside of me. The warmth spreading through me felt familiar, as if it were always there. It caused me to straighten my back, my hands no longer shaking against the demon's chest. Something was happening to me. Something unexplainable, unstoppable, so I didn't even try.

My eyes snapped to Zane's hazel eyes and he flinched. I wasn't sure what he saw in my face, but it caused him to drop his hand from my face. He stared at me in awe, as if seeing me for the first time. Confident in my newfound power over him, I pushed him away from me slightly. The hand on his chest touched something warm, and my eyes dropped to where I touched Zane's tattoo.

The binding sigil.

I didn't know how I did it or how I even knew what to do. I barely even thought about the sigil before it grew hot beneath my palm. The demon in Zane cried out and tried to pull away from me, but it was like our skin was fused together, my hand and his chest. His eyes jittered from side to side, panic making his heart beat faster under my hand.

For a brief moment, I focused on the beating of his heart. I could stop it as easily as I could save Zane. The temptation to do such a thing was right there. It was so overpowering I almost did it. I almost took

Zane's life, but in a split second, I changed my mind.

Not really aware of what I was doing, my mouth formed a single word. "Leave."

That one word sent a ripple of power from me and into Zane. Convulsions shuddered through Zane's body, his eyes rolling into the back of his head, and his mouth spread wide until it might tear. That darkness inside of me that wanted to kill Zane reveled in his pain.

Thankfully, it didn't last long. Zane's body tensed one last time, and his eyes widened before he crumpled in my arms.

I tried to hold on to him, but he was so heavy. He sank to the floor, and I quickly dropped off the table to grab him. Whatever power I had left me as I lifted his head and sat it on my lap. As I stroked his face, I worried over what had happened.

The longer the power wasn't awake inside of me, the more like myself I felt again. Which only made me quake with fear. Was it true? Was I something bad? The demon recognized me as something damned. Someone who deserved to be punished.

If what I just felt was anything to go by, then the woman I used to be, the one who had such hate in her heart, deserved to suffer. Trapped in a tower, suffering alone. Forever.

Chapter 16

Zane didn't wake up right away, and I didn't feel comfortable smacking him awake like Gage had, so I grabbed a book off the table and sat it on the ground, laying his head on top of it.

I should have gone for the others, but they would have questions. Those questions would lead to how I got rid of the demon, which would mean I'd have to tell them what I did. That wasn't something I was ready to talk about yet. Not to myself or anyone.

While I waited for Zane to come to, I flipped through the history book Zane had brought over. None of the events in the book really struck a chord with me, but the pictures seemed familiar somehow. The suits of armor, ladies giving tokens to their men, and the large castles their leaders lived in. They all tickled something in the back of my mind.

If I put that together with the dream I had, then Zane was right on the mark.

With the when solved, I had a better chance of figuring out who I was. They would have documented a prisoner they put in a tower which they then cloaked, right? I would think that was a bad enough punishment to warrant at least a paragraph?

The longer I read the history book, the less likely it seemed I would find anything about me or my tower. Picking up my coffee, I sighed and took a drink.

"Blech." I swallowed with a grimace. Coffee might taste good hot but cold, I might as well be drinking cold tar. Sitting my cup down with an aggravated grunt, I grabbed another book on the history of the mages. I had only just flipped to the first page when my eyes slid over to Zane and then back to my cup. An idea came to my head. An impossible idea that couldn't, in all likeliness, ever happen.

But why not? Zane had changed the flavor of my coffee with just a wave of his hand, why shouldn't I be able to warm it back up? After all, it couldn't be that much harder than banishing a demon, could it?

Picking my cup up, I sat it in front of me and stared down into it. I really had no idea what I was doing. Zane hadn't said anything when he had changed it, so it would figure I wouldn't need any kind of magic words to do what I wanted to do.

I placed my hand over the cup and thought about warming it up. I stared at it for a long time, but nothing happened. No tingles or anything like with Zane. Sighing in defeat, I dropped my hand and went back to my book.

It was a stupid idea anyway.

Instead of just blindingly reading the history which could take forever, I searched for anything that had to do with the Middle Ages or an evil woman about to marry a king. Unfortunately, there wasn't a lot of concrete information about the time period, with the mages staying concealed during the humans' reign. Many of them acted as advisers to the human kings, pretending to tell their fortunes and help them in great battles. Most of it was a lot of nonsense. The mages didn't want the humans to win anything other than a quick death. It seemed like not much has changed in that aspect from then to now.

I had just about given up when I found a passage about a king named Midas and his quest for gold. During his quest, he had come across a mage who gifted him the ability to turn anything he wanted into gold. Many people thought the ability came from Midas himself, but what they didn't know was that the mage had given Midas a young woman. She was the one who created the gold for Midas. Eventually, Midas fell for the young woman and made her his queen.

Eagerly turning the page for more, I frowned when I only found an entry about the beginning of the Dark Ages. Quickly, I returned to the previous page, reading back over it for anything I might have missed, but I hadn't. It was the same story I'd read the first time.

Growling in frustration, I snapped the book closed and shoved it away. Not realizing how close it was to the edge, the book fell off the table and landed on the ground with a loud thud.

Letting out a huff, I leaned down to pick it up, but a groan from Zane distracted me. My eyes moved over to where he lay and watched as his eyes fluttered open. I hurried over to his side, while he groaned and grabbed his head in his hands.

"Zane, are you alright?" I asked, helping him sit up.

His red hair curtained around his face and he had to push it back just so he could blink up at me. Realizing his glasses were missing, Zane squinted and leaned in. "Eva?"

Suddenly, remembering his glasses, I let go of him and ran over to the table. I snatched them up from where the demon had tossed them and hurried back over to him. "Here." I set his glasses on his nose and smiled softly. "Is that better?"

"Much, thank you." Zane returned my smile, but then frowned as he took in where he sat. "Why am I on the floor?"

I contemplated what to tell him. Obviously, the demon has taken over before, but I didn't want to let Zane know what the demon almost did, let alone what he had said to me. I opened and shut my mouth, feeling a bit like a fish out of water, but Zane seemed to catch on a lot quicker than I would have expected.

"The demon took over again, didn't it?" he asked quietly. Before I could answer him, he sighed long and hard. His voice was filled with so much anguish as he gathered up his hair that I couldn't lie to him.

"Yes."

Zane stared up at me, worry pinching his brows. "Did he hurt you? What did he say?"

I shook my head and quickly said, "No, he didn't hurt me. I swear." I peered down at him and then added softly, "He doesn't like you much, does he?"

I didn't think Zane would want to know what almost happened between us. It would make him feel more horrible than he already did. I hoped talking about his relationship with the demon might dissuade his questions about what truly happened just a bit ago.

Zane closed his eyes for a moment and then let out a bitter laugh. "No, I suppose he wouldn't. After all, I'm the one who trapped him here."

"Wait, I thought he was the one who trapped you?" I cocked my head to the side, trying to remember what he had said before.

"No, not really. He has access to my body and mind, but he can't go back to wherever he came from. He's stuck in the recesses of my mind until I let my guard down enough that he can break through." He huffed and dragged a hand over his face. "Which seems to be happening a lot around you."

"He did seem overly interested in me." I shrugged, leaving out the parts about how I should be punished and the other unpleasant things he had said and tried to do.

"If he said anything that hurt your feelings or scared you, I am sorry." He reached out as if to touch me, but dropped his hand, his eyes going to the floor. "It's not a representation of my own thoughts, so you know. I have no control over what he says or does when he takes over. Nor do I know what he's done."

"I know." My words were quiet and full of guilt. I wished I could tell him what happened but then I would have to tell him how I stopped him. Something I wasn't ready to do. Not with how they treated humans. I wasn't sure how'd they'd treat a human with magic.

We sat there silently for a few moments before Zane stood and brushed himself off. He leaned down with a small smile and offered me a hand to stand. Taking it, he drew me up until we were a hair's breadth away from each other. Unlike when the demon had done it, my heartbeat raced for a completely different reason.

Zane's eyes settled on mine, and his hot breath brushed my face. "Unfortunately, it isn't a two-way street. He can see in my mind a lot more fully than I can see into his, both a blessing and a curse." He grinned for a moment before he grew serious once more. "Did he tell you anything about me?"

I could tell he was anxious about what the demon could have possibly told me. It made me start to think that what the demon had said about Zane wanting me might not have been completely untrue. Wetting my lips, I shook my head slightly. "No, nothing. Just taunted me and made threats. He really seemed into scaring me and punishing you."

Relief came swift to his face, and he bobbed his head. "Good. Good." He paused for a moment before pushing his glasses back up his face. "How were you able to get rid of him anyway?"

This was the part I didn't want to talk about. Not only because of the power I couldn't explain, but because of the brief moment where I wanted to crush Zane's heart rather than save it. Not sure what to say, I lied.

"I didn't," I blurted out and then hurried to add, "I mean, he must have gotten bored because he left on his own," I added a shrug on to the end, hoping to add some realness to the story.

Zane seemed taken back by my explanation, as if it wasn't at all what he was expecting. Hell, I didn't even know what he should have expected. Last time, it took Gage's physical warning to make the demon leave, obviously just getting bored wasn't as profound of a threat. I just hoped Zane didn't ask any more about the matter.

"That seems unlikely," Zane finally proclaimed, his brows furrowing as he stared at me. I forced myself not to fidget and give myself away. I didn't think telling him I'd used some kind of power to make his demon flee was the best of ideas. Nope. Not at all.

"Well, he did," I assured him, and left it at that.

Frowning but not prying any further, Zane stepped away from me and turned to the books on the table. "I see you have continued your research while I was out."

"Yes, I was trying to see if anything stood out." I sighed more for the sake of Zane changing the subject than being disappointed that I hadn't found anything else.

Zane flipped through the book I had been reading and asked, "And did it?"

I thought about King Midas and the dream I had and then shook my head. I had my suspicions, but nothing concrete. It didn't make sense to tell him what I thought until I knew for sure it wouldn't land me back in my tower. "No, I didn't find anything."

Shifting through the books on the table, Zane muttered under his breath too low for me to make out. I moved over to the table as well, picking up the book I had found about King Midas. Leaning against the side of the table, I hesitated for a moment before asking, "Have you heard of King Midas?"

"King Midas?" Zane's face scrunched up. "You mean the guy with the golden hand?"

Not sure what he was talking about, but close enough to the story I'd read, I pressed, "Uh, yeah. Him. What happened to him?"

"It's a myth. A tragic story really." He gathered up his books, shoving them back into his bag. "This rich king wanted even more money than he already had and prayed to the gods for the ability to make gold with a single touch. Unfortunately, the gods were petty, and Midas soon realized that the gift he had been given was actually a curse."

"Why?" I questioned, on the edge of my seat to hear what he had to say. The woman had been a curse? Why? She was giving him what he wanted, wasn't she?

Zane started braiding his hair back as he spoke, my eyes mesmerized by the movements of his fingers as well as his words. "Well, the power didn't just turn what he wanted into gold, but everything else as well. His food, his pets, even his daughter." I forced myself not to react to his words. Midas had a daughter, just like the one in my dream.

"What happened then?" My heart was in my throat as I urged him to continue. Even as I asked, I had a feeling I didn't want to know, but I needed to. I had so few answers that anything was better than being in the dark.

Zane shrugged. "There are a few different endings. Some say that he starved to death because of his gift. Others say he prayed to his god to take the gift back and he did, as well as turning everything he had changed into gold back to the way they were. Including his daughter."

"I like the second version better," I told him with a relieved sigh, though my thoughts weren't really on what Zane had said.

Smiling slightly, Zane chuckled. "The story is supposed to be a cautionary tale of being careful what you wish for. Either ending teaches that."

I nodded like I was listening. The god that had given Midas the power might have very well been the mage. Obviously, they kept out the part about the woman. Probably thought it sounded better for the king to have all the power.

"And his wife?" I asked, trying to make my voice sound as normal as possible.

Zane's brow furrowed. "I don't think I ever heard anything about a queen. I mean, I'd assume he had one since he had a daughter, but no one ever talks about her. Why do you want to know?"

"Oh, nothing." I shook my head and smiled. "I just saw something about him in one of the books and was wondering."

His lips curved up into an amused grin. "There is no shame in wanting to learn, especially someone in your position. You probably have a million questions as it is. I want you to feel free to ask me anything you want. Anything at all. I won't judge you, promise." He crossed his fingers over his heart. Right above the tattoo on his chest.

I ducked my head to hide my face, more for the guilt weighing on my heart than bashfulness. "Okay. I'll remember that."

"Eva," Zane started, moving closer to me. "About the demon..."

Whatever he was about to say was cut off when Gage burst through the library door. Straightening as if we had been caught doing something we shouldn't, I put a few more inches between us.

"Gage?" Zane asked, adjusting his eyepieces. "What is it?"

Gage shot a suspicious look my way, which made the urge to stick my tongue out at him almost unbearable. Taking the more mature road, I crossed my arms over my chest and glared back.

Not at all affected by my glower, Gage answered Zane. "We have been summoned to stand before the Council. It seems someone," his eyes darted toward me with disapproval, "has drawn their attention."

Zane looked at me and said, "Don't worry. They're not as big and bad as they seem. I'm sure they just want to check on you and see if you remembered anything."

Gage snorted.

"Of course." I ignored Gage and agreed with Zane. "I'm sure it will be fine."

Throwing the strap of his bag over his shoulder, Zane started for the door. "Besides, the Headquarters has one of the best libraries in the area. You are bound to find something about yourself there."

"Of course." I nodded, following after him, well aware of Gage's eyes on me the whole time. "We'll find something." When I said 'we' I meant 'me,' because at the rate I was going, I didn't want them to know anything about my past. And if Gage or Blake found out first, I had no doubt I'd be back up in my tower faster than I could say refrigerator.

Chapter 17

I followed Gage and Zane out of the library and through the house. Adam exited his office just as we passed by, and the look on his face was not encouraging. He fell in line with us as we made our way to the front of the house.

My hand itched to reach out and touch Adam, to ask the question no one was asking. But I didn't know him well enough to be so forward, and I feared the answer to the question. I curled my fingers into a fist to keep myself from touching him.

"Wait," I called out making them stop and look back to me. Zane and Adam with concern and Gage with suspicion. Licking my lips, I tried to think of some reason not to go to see the Mage Council. "I…uh…I need to relieve my bladder."

I spun on my heel and darted toward the nearest bathroom, closing and locking the door behind me. My back pressed against the wall I took in several long cleansing breaths.

I could do this. I could totally do this. My fingers laced in front of me and then unlaced before I relaced them again. Then I switched from crossing my arms and pacing to chewing on my nail.

A soft knock on the bathroom door had my heart jumping in my throat. I started to the door and then stopped as a soft concerned voice asked, "Eva, are you alright?"

Adam. Of course, he would be worried about me. This whole household – except for Gage and sometimes Blake – had been nothing but kind to me and I was about to screw it up for all of them. I couldn't do this.

"I'll be just a second," I called out and then turned back to the toilet. I put the lid down and sat down, my eyes darting to the door and back. I waited for Adam to leave but he didn't.

"You know, Eva." Adam's voice projected through the door far more than it should have and I wondered if it was something kind of spell. "There's nothing to worry about. We won't let anything happen to you. I promise. You are in safe hands with us."

"I know," I stuttered out and then forced myself to take a deep breath before clearing my throat. "I mean, I'm alright. Just I think what I ate didn't agree with my stomach."

Adam chuckled before adding, "Well, I think all of us have come down with something just when the council ordered for us to appear before them. I remember this one time. I was in the middle of having sex and Master Tuck appeared in the middle of my bedroom to take me in for an emergency meeting." He snickered and I could just imagine the smile on his face even as mine went beet red. "From then on, I put a no-teleporting charm around the house. Though, I was pretty sure Master Tuck would never pop in unannounced again."

I let out a nervous laugh. "I can imagine."

"So, what I guess I'm trying to say…is that it's normal to be nervous. We've all been there." Adam sighed and the door sounded like he was scratching a nail against the door. "But you'll have us there with you. You won't be alone. You'll never be alone again," he added on a low note as if this was all about something else entirely.

Standing from the toilet, I didn't even bother washing my hands. The charade was up before it even began. Slowly walking to the door, I unlocked it and opened it a crack. The door pushed open further and Adam's eyes met mine a small smile on his lips.

"There's our girl. Feeling better?" He arched a brow and I couldn't fight back the tugging at the edges of my lips.

"Yes," I nodded and let him lead me out of the bathroom. We walked the short way down the hall and stopped by Gage and Zane. At Zane's concerned look, I offered him a reassuring smile. "I'm fine now. We can go."

Taking me at my word, Zane led the way out of the house. Outside of the house the twins waited for us by the car. Luke's lips were turned down in a frown, his hands wringing his robe in his tight grasp. Blake simply looked annoyed, as per usual. I was sure being summoned by the council didn't worry him the way it did the others. He probably only cared that it interrupted his day rather than the fact that I might be in danger.

"Let's get this over with." Blake scowled, crossing his arms over his chest.

Adam shot him a warning look before opening the car door, ushering me inside with a small smile. "Don't worry, I'm sure it's nothing."

I smiled back at him, though I didn't feel very reassured. I ducked into the car and slid across the leather seats to curl up in the corner by the opposite door. Adam climbed in after finding a seat across from me. His eyes darted to me every few moments from behind the book he had pulled out.

Gage slipped in next, as silent as death, and took his position beside Adam, making the inside of the car seem even smaller than it already felt. His menacing presence did nothing to ease my fears. I shifted uncomfortably and tried to move even closer to the door.

Next to enter was Luke, who happily sat beside me, his thigh pressing against my own. The cheery grin on his lips made me sag a bit in relief. It couldn't be that bad if he was in a good mood. A small bit of hope was determined to wiggle its way back into my heart.

Zane and Blake were the last to enter, shutting the door behind them. With Blake's permanent attitude, the atmosphere in the already tension-filled car reached an all-time level of thickness. I was surprised we could breathe at all.

The car began to move beneath us, something that still felt strange to me. From what I discovered with Zane, cars were not something I was used to. A horse-drawn carriage was more my speed, and I imagined it wasn't quite as smooth of a ride as the contraption they used for transportation.

Instead of focusing on the torturous quiet in the car, I turned my gaze to the window. The windows were clear on the inside, so I could easily see those walking along the streets, though I knew they couldn't see me. The first time we went down this street, I hadn't been paying much attention. My head was still befuddled with the spell of the tower, and I hadn't really cared what was going on, only that I was free.

The second time we went down this street, I was with Luke. I'd been so excited to get out of the house, I didn't even know that I should have been watching those passing us by. It also didn't help that Luke had entertained me with stories and jokes, so my attention wasn't exactly on the right things.

Now, however, I knew what I was looking for. The humans dressed in their dull clothing, their eyes down on the ground as they hurried to get to where they were going. There wasn't any open oppression. None of the mages spat on the humans or threw things at them.

No, the kind of oppression that poisoned this world was the worst kind. Indifference. The mages didn't even find the humans worthy of their attention. They acted as if they didn't even notice them. They were nothing more than the ghosts who washed their clothing, made their food, and cleaned their homes.

It was surprising the men even bothered to pay any attention to me. I was a lowly human. They shouldn't care about me. I should be the annoyance they wanted to get rid of and yet...and yet they looked at me like I was something more.

"What are you thinking about?" Luke nudged me with his elbow, breaking me out of my thoughts.

I offered him a weak smile. "Nothing, just wondering what the council wants."

Adam gave me a curious look, but didn't say anything as Luke grinned and threw an arm over my shoulders. "Ah, don't worry your pretty little head about them. They're just a bunch of old farts who like to make a big deal about everything."

"Lucas," Gage warned with a glared.

"What?" Luke held his hands open and shrugged. "It's true."

"Still," Zane shook his head disapprovingly, "you shouldn't speak about them in such a manner. It's disrespectful."

"Not to mention stupid," Blake scoffed, gesturing out the window. "They have their little spies everywhere. Who knows who's listening to you bad mouthing them?"

Luke tensed slightly at Blake's warning, but didn't stop smiling. "Big deal. Those namby-pamby mages wouldn't dare make a move on us, not with Adam in the running for Arch Mage."

"Arch Mage?" My brows rose as I turned my attention to Adam.

Adam shifted uncomfortably in his seat, but didn't put his book up. When he didn't answer, Zane pushed his eyepieces up his face and cleared his throat. "An Arch Mage is the highest level one can achieve. It requires years of practice, wisdom, and—"

"And a hefty amount of tolerance for political bullshit," Blake interjected with a sarcastic chuckle, earning him a glower from Adam.

"Anyways," Zane continued with an exasperated sigh, "Adam is one of the youngest mages in the running. You have to be a master mage to even be considered to run."

"And you're a master mage?" I asked Adam.

Adam glanced up from his book to meet my gaze. "Yes, I am."

"Adam is the youngest mage to make master ever." Luke beamed with pride as if it were his own achievement he was proclaiming.

Rolling his eyes, Adam turned his eyes back to his book. There was more to this than the elusive leader of the group was saying. If he really was that powerful, why let the council push him around? Also, why be so tight-lipped about it? If I knew I had that much power, I wouldn't just stay quiet about it. I'd be making sure everyone knew not to make me mad.

As if knowing my train of thought, without looking up from his book, Adam said, "It takes more than power to be a master mage. It takes knowing when to use that power and when to keep it quiet."

Zane nodded in agreement, brushing his red braid over his shoulder. "Hence why Master Tuck is his only opposition."

The image of Master Tuck and his greedy eyes caused me to shudder. I couldn't imagine how much worse the world would be with him in charge. At least Adam had some semblance of respect for others, even humans. Master Tuck hadn't hidden his distaste for my heritage. No, with him in charge, things could only get worse, not better.

"As you can imagine, Master Tuck doesn't like Adam too much because of that," Zane continued, and then Luke added, "And the fact that Adam made master far sooner than he did."

"Yes." Zane nodded. "That as well. Which means we can only assume the reason we are being called to the council is because of Master Tuck."

"He's got his panties in a twist to make Adam look bad." Blake sniffed. "And you are just the thing he needs to show the council how reckless and immature Adam is."

"That's not true," Luke snapped at his brother, and then turned to me. "Don't listen to Blake, he's just an asshole." He turned his glare toward his twin.

"He's right," Gage announced, breaking his silence. "You are just the thing Tuck needs to get Adam kicked out of the race, making him Arch Mage by default." His eyes settled on me, weighing heavily upon me.

"Gage." Adam's voice was hard and full of something I couldn't describe, but it made Gage stop talking. To me, Adam said, "Don't worry, it will take more than that to knock

221

me down. Master Tuck will be grasping at straws."

"That's right." Zane leaned forward, his cross hanging down between his legs. "Besides, we don't know for sure that's what the council is calling us about. For all we know, it might just want to meet you." A slow smile curved up his lips, making something warm shift inside of me. "After all, you are the greatest phenomenon since the meteorite landed."

I nodded and smiled, but it was forced. They were all hurrying to reassure me, but their words were empty to me. Guilt ate at me. What Blake and Gage had said was true. In a world where humans weren't even considered worthy of respect, I was a huge, glaring thorn in Master Tuck's side and a reason to point fingers at Adam. His harboring me, not letting Master Tuck take me, showed he wasn't the sort of person the council would want in charge.

I could just imagine what the council would have to say about Adam's weakness for the little human girl without her memories or any clue of who and what she was. Let alone if they found out that this human had powers as well. Then, there would be no telling what they would do, not just to me but to all of them.

The car stopped abruptly, and everyone quieted. Adam closed his book, and with a twist of his wrist, it was gone. "We're here."

Chapter 18

The door was opened for us by a mage with a pale blue cloak. His eyes were down as we exited the car, except when I passed by. The curious look in his eyes made me shift closer to Luke.

We made our way away from the car and up a long red carpet. There were blue, light-filled barriers on either side of the carpet with people standing behind them. Some I recognized from the tower with their metal sticks and floating eyes. Others were mages with signs, shouting such a multitude of things that I had to focus hard to pick out just one.

"Humans came first!"

"The council is corrupt!'

And on and on the sordid protests came. At least some actually cared about humans.

Though the amount of those protesting was small, it built on that small ball of hope I had inside of me. My eyes drew up to the large white building with a red cross and branch on the side. I didn't need to be told this was the Mage Headquarters. The ambiance and protesters told me that much.

"Come on, Eva." Luke wrapped his arm around my shoulders, ushering me away from the crowd. "Don't move away from my side, alright?"

I glanced up at him, confused. "Why?"

"Because there are those who would hurt you just to hurt us. Or just because you are human. And I couldn't handle anything happening to you." His lips twisted in a grimace as his eyes shifted around us, even as we passed through a heavily guarded entrance.

The inside of the building was just as cold and hard as the outside. Everything was made of glass or some kind of magical material that glittered along the walls. Another large red cross with a branch decorated the wall here and every pillar we passed on our way through the front.

The front had a sitting area that we bypassed. There weren't any people waiting today. I was glad for it. Any more eyes on me and I might burst into flames. The ones on me already held enough disgust at my presence as it were.

"This way." A mage with dark green robes motioned down a hallway.

Gage glared at the mage, causing him to pale. "We know the way."

Adam placed a hand on Gage's shoulder, giving the mage a smile that made his eyes squint. "Thank you, but we can find our way from here."

"But ...but..." The mage started, his eyes darting from Gage to Adam. "I am supposed to escort you."

"Then by all means." Adam waved a hand forward, gesturing for the mage to continue walking.

With one more cautious look toward Gage, the mage nodded and started down the hallway once more. Every once in awhile, he would start to say something but then stop, his eyes going to Gage again. He'd swallow hard and quicken his footsteps as if the mere presence of Gage frightened him.

I wasn't surprised. The large man could be intimidating. He hadn't said more than a few words to me at a time. Most of the words he had said were to the others. Out of all of them, I felt that if it came down to it—if it were between them and me—Gage would happily throw me to the wolves.

"Relax," Luke muttered in my ear, his hand rubbing up and down my arm. "You're going to be fine."

I tried to relax, I really did, but with the unknown before me and a secret of my own to keep, it was kind of hard to find one's breath. For Luke's sake, I forced my back to unstiffen and to erase the pinching frown on my face. Maybe if I pretended I was alright, I'd begin to feel it.

One could hope.

The mage leading us stopped before a set of double doors. They were large and imposing, as if the atmosphere of the place wasn't enough to frighten potential visitors. That, and the guards on either side of the doors, their faces hard as stone, expressionless and as sharp as the swords at their sides. For a brief second, one of the guard's eyes slid over me, his face hardening even more. I shifted closer to Luke, grasping onto his cloak as if it might protect me.

It was a stupid and silly thought. From what they have told me of the council and from the fear on the streets, nothing the men could do would save me from the council if they wanted me gone. I just prayed that time never came.

As the doors opened for us, a masculine voice called out, "Presenting Master Adam, Cleric Zane, Conjuror Blake, Sentinel Gage, and Healer Lucas." The voice paused, before adding with distaste, "And the untested human, Eva."

The names attached to the others' names were intriguing and definitely something I would have to ask about later. At the moment, my attention was too focused on the imposing group of five sitting high upon a wood-like throne. They were so high up that I had to lean my head back to see them, their feet more than ten feet from the ground.

How did they even get on those things?

"Master Adam," an elderly man with a kind face and tired eyes said, sitting in the middle of the group. I hoped against hope that this was the Arch Mage Heizer. He wasn't dressed any more finely than the others, but his chair did hold a bit more decoration to it than the others.

At being singled out, Adam bent to one knee before the council. "Arch Mage, we have come as you have summoned us."

Heizer threw his head back and chuckled. "So formal, as always, Master Adam." He gestured a worn and wrinkled hand for Adam to stand up. "You know how I feel about bowing, Grandson."

Adam stood and rubbed the back of his neck, a bit sheepish. "Old habits."

Luke leaned over to whisper, "Oh, yeah. I forgot to mention Heizer is Adam's grandfather."

I didn't tell Luke I'd already figured that out by Heizer's slip. Instead, I just nodded, keeping my mouth closed. Hopefully, that would keep them from remembering me. Doubtful.

"How are you doing?" Heizer asked, his eyes twinkling with mirth. "I heard you have had quite a bit of excitement as of late." His gaze moved from Adam to where I stood by Luke. Damn.

Adam didn't glance back at me or acknowledge his grandfather's hinting. "I'm doing as well as can be in these times, and there's never too much excitement for me to handle, as you know." I could barely see the side of Adam's face, but there was a hint of a smile there that said he wasn't falling for his games.

"Are we going to talk niceties all day, or are we going to talk about that thing in the room?" A woman with a large amount of white hair piled on her head pointed a finger at me, a sneer on her lips.

The others on their thrones, except Heizer, began to nod and whisper in agreement. Heizer's lips pressed into a thin line as he stared down at his grandson as if some kind of unspoken exchange were happening. Whatever they were talking about, I didn't get it, but a moment later, Adam turned to me.

Holding a hand out, he met my gaze as if trying to warn me. "Come, Eva."

I would usually be eager to take that hand, but not this time. This time, everything in me wanted to run the other direction. I shot a glance at Luke, who frowned, and released me though with reluctance. As I stepped away from Luke and toward Adam, I cast a quick look to Zane who didn't look all that encouraging. I didn't bother looking at Gage or Blake, who I knew wouldn't care what I wanted either way.

When my hand finally found Adam's, it was like all the sound in the room had been sucked up. All eyes were on me as he drew me forward to the waiting eyes of the council. I didn't know what I was supposed to do. Curtsey? Bend a knee like Adam did? Instead, I did nothing.

"Come closer, child," Heizer instructed me with a come-hither gesture of his hand. "Do not be afraid. We wish you no ill will."

I wanted to snort but refrained. He might not wish me harm, but those sitting at his side sure didn't share that same sentiment. To them, I was a problem. I could see it in the tightness around their mouths, the annoyance in their eyes. To them, I was something that should be disposed of, burned to ash, not paraded around.

Forcing my opinions to myself, I moved forward as asked, keeping my eyes on the Arch Mage. His eyes clinically scanned over my form as if he were trying to figure me out, not see beneath my clothing. I was thankful for the former, though I hoped he couldn't read minds.

"Your name is Eva?" he asked at last.

My mouth dropped open, and I started to answer, but then paused. Should I answer him? What was the proper protocol? Then I decided to forget about it. They wanted to see me, the mysterious human they wanted to stare and point at. So, that would be what they got.

"Yes, that's my name." I straightened my spine and put my hands down by my sides, refusing to cower before them. I might not remember much about my past, but I knew in my heart that I was never someone to submit because I was told to.

"I have been informed that my grandson and his fellow mages found you in a tower in

Old Central Park." He watched me closely, his eyes searching for a lie.

I wasn't sure if I was supposed to answer him, he hadn't posed it as a question, but I answered anyway. "That's right. Though I'm not sure what Old Central Park is. I only know about my tower."

"*Your* tower?" This question came from one of the men on the left side of Heizer. His eyes were less beady and more quizzical than the others.

I smirked and shrugged. "Well, when you live somewhere for as long as I have, you have to figure it's yours by some point." My answer caused Heizer and a few others to chuckle, most of those laughs coming from behind me.

"And how long were you in that tower?" the same mage asked, his head tilting to the side so that his dark hair fell over his face. He was significantly younger than the others around him, something that probably got mentioned on numerous occasions.

I started to answer, but Zane stepped up beside me. "After some research and what recollection Eva has, we have determined she was put in the tower around the Middle Ages, maybe even shortly after the Necronite fell to Earth."

There was a bit of commotion from the council after Zane's announcement. Many of them said things that sounded like I was more of a threat than a mystery. It seemed my small claim to fame was going to be short-lived.

Chapter 19

"So, by my calculations, you have been in that tower for over a thousand years," Heizer speculated, his eyes zeroing on me, ignoring the arguments of his fellow council members.

I ducked my head. "Yes. We think so."

Sitting back in his chair, Heizer shook his head in disbelief. "How are you still alive, let alone sane?"

Zane started to answer for me again, but I beat him to it. I didn't want the council to think I was hiding behind my rescuers. "I understand that there was a spell involved keeping me in a form of stasis, which allowed me to live—if you could really call it living—without food or drink, putting my body in a perpetual state of limbo. As far as sane?" I grinned slightly. "That's still up for debate."

The groan from behind me made me a bit worried that I'd gone too far, but Heizer didn't seem particularly worried, so I left it alone. I stood before them as they argued amongst themselves. Heizer stayed silent, his focus completely on me.

"We should take her to the university," a man with eyeglasses and a hungry gaze started, the want in his eyes was purely academic. "Surely, they would be able to figure out how this is possible."

"They would cut her to pieces there," the young council member argued, a frown marring his face at the very idea. "We have long since banned human experimentation. To bring it up now..." He shook his head in disgust.

The hungry one didn't seem bothered by it. "But this is a scientific and magical miracle. We can't just let her walk around out there in the world. Who knows what secrets lie within her?"

The woman from before snorted, crossing her legs. "I don't care about her magical secrets. I care more to know why she was put there to begin with. Someone went to great lengths to make sure she wasn't found. There must be a reason why."

"I concur!" Another female, her bright red hair in two braids and sitting next to the younger one, held a hand up. Her eyes found me, and there was nothing but envy and malice there. "Who knows what kind of a danger she is to the populace?"

"She's not a danger to anyone." This came from Adam, who moved up to stand beside me. "She has stayed at our home and has not shown any signs of aggression or anything that would indicate that she is anything other than a human without her memories."

"But what if they come back?" the redheaded woman asked, but it came out as more of a hiss. I noticed then that her eyes were a golden green with slits for pupils. And they thought I was a danger to society!

"Then all the better," Heizer interjected, causing the rest of the council to calm down. "I think we would all sleep easier knowing exactly who this young lady is, including Eva herself. Don't you agree?" He glanced around the council who all nodded, though some were more disgruntled than others.

I thought we were done, and we might get to go home, but the woman with the white hair asked, "What about what Master Tuck told us?"

Tuck, of course. I shouldn't have hoped that he didn't have anything to do with this. The men had already warned me about it. Just because he wasn't present didn't mean that he didn't have a hand in this situation.

I could tell that Heizer was not happy about his fellow council member's reminder. I wasn't either. It would have been nice to forget it altogether so I could go home and get away from these vultures.

"We have no proof what Master Tuck has stated has any merit." Heizer tried to dissuade the subject, but they wouldn't be convinced.

"How does her very presence and demeanor not prove it?" the redhead hissed, her eyes looking me up and down. "She stands before us as if she were our equal, rather than a lowly human. Master Adam and his group have obviously shown favoritism toward the human for her to speak so blatantly to her betters."

My teeth ground together, and I started to take a step forward to tell her exactly what I thought about her, but Adam took my hand in his, his grip tight. It was that slight pinch that caused me to keep my mouth shut.

"I apologize for Eva's bluntness." The sincerity in his voice made even me believe that he thought I was out of line. I bristled, but another squeeze of my hand kept me quiet. "As you've found out for yourself, she's not from a time where humans were seen as the weaker group. We must give her some liberties until she is eased into her place."

The redhead scoffed, turning her face into her hand. "More like you have been taking liberties of your own."

I could feel the men behind me shift as one. They did not like her accusation, not one bit. When her face blanched, I almost smiled up at her. Almost.

The man with glasses shifted and tapped his fingers on the arm of his throne. "Giving her freedoms she would not otherwise have would only start unhealthy habits. You must teach her from the start what is expected of her and who she serves." His eyes narrowed on me as if he could change me on the spot.

"Understandable." Adam nodded, his lips pressed tightly together. "We will begin right away on rehabilitating Eva to her position. You have my word on that."

Heizer frowned at his grandson's words. "And the others?"

Zane shifted beside me, clearly unhappy with how the proceedings were going. "We will do everything in our power to make Eva a reputable member of our society. The next time you meet her, she will no longer pose any threat."

I gaped at him. The way Zane talked about me made me feel as if I were a pet that needed to be chained up and taught a lesson, though I shouldn't have been surprised. The way the council talked about me pretty much implied that very notion.

"Caoins?"

The twins moved up behind me at Heizer's question. Luke pressed against my back with Blake next to him, but barely touching me. I should have felt safe with them all around me, but at that moment, I wanted to be as far away from them all as possible.

"I understand," Luke answered behind me.

"I've been saying the very thing from the start," Blake growled, earning him a nudge from his brother. Apparently, Blake had no qualms about displaying his distaste for me in public or throwing his fellow mages under the horse.

"Very well," Heizer sighed as if he were tired from the whole ordeal. I noticed they never asked Gage his opinion on the matter, but then again, he was the council's assassin. He probably jumped when they said jump.

Adam tugged me around the group and toward the door. Apparently, we had been dismissed. The grip on my arm didn't loosen as we hurried through the corridors. I tried to ask questions but was shushed by Adam and then by Zane.

When we left the building, Adam dropped my arm and headed for the car. This time he didn't open the door for me or wait for me to go first. He entered without a word, followed by the others, leaving me last to go. Befuddled by the group's sudden change in personalities, I hesitated to get in the car.

Blake leaned out and shouted, "Get in already."

Jumping in place, I shot a glance around me before crawling inside. The only place left was beside Blake with Zane across from me. I opened my mouth to start asking questions the moment the door shut.

"Not yet," Adam warned, causing me to clamp my mouth firmly shut.

It wasn't until we had been on the road for a good five minutes before Adam turned his eyes to mine. "Well, that did not go as I had hoped, but we have bought ourselves some time."

The others relaxed slightly at Adam's words, but I was still confused as ever. What had he expected to happen? What time did they need?

"Of course, the hardest part will be for Eva. You are already out of your depth, and I apologize in advance, but the coming days are necessary for not only your survival but our own." He glanced around the group, who had all grown sullen.

"But I don't know what's going on. What will happen to me if I don't do what they want?" I searched around the inside of the car as if it had the answer I needed. "And what about finding out who I am?"

"Never fear, Eva." Zane patted me on the arm. "We will still figure out who you are and how you came to be in that tower."

At the moment, those things weren't as important as the questions they didn't answer. I had learned a lot of things in my short span of time with the council and none of them boded well for me. I could only pray that what the others had said was more for appearance's sake and not being taken to heart.

Chapter 20

The ride home was quiet. Everyone was lost in their own thoughts. I knew my mind was reeling. I was supposed to start acting like the humans here, but how could I do that and find out who I really was?

I didn't expect things to change suddenly. Zane's words had given me some kind of hope that they were just saying those horrible things so they wouldn't get in trouble. Then we would all go back home, and things would be like normal.

Except they weren't.

The moment we arrived back home, Gage marched me through the house, his hand on my elbow the entire time. When they had decided he would take charge, I didn't know, nor did I care. I only wanted to know why. I searched for the others, my eyes pleading, but they had all made themselves scarce. It was only the assassin and me. Gage's presence only made my hope shrivel up inside me.

He led me down the hallway that led to my room, but instead of stopping, we bypassed it, going down a set of stairs I never even noticed until now. The light grew dimmer. The further we descended, the colder it felt, and the higher my anxiety climbed. My breathing became erratic, my pulse pounding in my ears.

No. No. Not again. I won't be locked up again.

I tried to pull my arm out of Gage's grasp, but he held on tight, not even bothering to spare me a glance. I jerked and clawed at his hand, but he didn't so much as flinch.

"Let me go, let me go," I shouted. However, my words fell on deaf ears.

When the door came into view, a pathetic whimper fell from my lips. My head shook from side to side. I didn't need to see the other side of that door to know that it would be a prison. Just like the tower. I couldn't go back there. I wouldn't survive. I barely had the first time.

Gage stopped us before the door and pulled a key from his pocket. He inserted it into the door and turned it, the sound of a turning lock creaking through the stone hallway. Shoving the door open, he tried to whip me around, but I dug my heels in.

"Please, Gage," I begged, grabbing at his large biceps. "Please don't put me in there. I won't survive. I'll be good. I'll do what they want, I promise."

For a moment, Gage's usually expressionless face softened, the first sign of how much it distressed him to be there coming through. Then, as if remembering himself, his face scrunched up into a scowl, and he shoved me into the room without a word.

I hit the cool stone ground with a smack, my hands barely catching me before I landed on my face. I only had a moment to register the pain before I was back on my feet, but I wasn't fast enough to keep the door from slamming shut. The sound ricocheted through the room and into my heart, where it shattered any semblance of sanity I had into fragments.

I collapsed against the wooden door, my breathing increasing to the point I thought I might pass out. I closed my eyes and forced myself to focus on my breathing. In and out, nice and slow.

When I felt like I wasn't about to faint on the spot, I opened my eyes. Just as I feared. The room was about the size of my tower chamber except it was worse. While having a bed to sleep on was a big improvement, the lack of a window and real light made it infinitely worse.

Moving across the room with small, shaky steps, I fell onto the bed, burying my face in the musty pillow. Just when I started to wonder why I hadn't cried, the tears began to fall. At first, slow, quiet tears fell before the utter betrayal of it all settled into me, turning into racking sobs.

I didn't know when I fell asleep, whether before I stopped crying or during. While I knew I was still in my new prison, my mind was somewhere else. Somewhere I remembered all too easily.

I was back in the tower. This time though I wasn't alone.

A woman stood before me. Her hair, as dark as the night sky, was twisted into an elaborate updo, and a crown sat on top of her head. Her black eyes glared down at me as if ai were the cause of all of her woes. Based on the way her bloodred lips curled into a sneer, I knew it was true.

I sat on the ground, my legs sprawled out in front of me. I tugged on my arms, but they wouldn't budge from the cool manacles chaining me to the wall. My teeth ground together, and I let out a low growl.

"You won't get away with this," I could hear myself say, but there was something wrong with my voice. I'd never heard myself sound this way before, a burning tone filled with bitterness and rage. Nothing like I sounded now.

What had caused me to be so angry? Well, being locked in a tower probably had a lot to do with it.

The woman in front of me laughed, her head thrown back and a hand up to her mouth. The sound of it bounced off the walls, filling the room with it. I hated that sound. If I were free, I would dig my nails into her throat and rip it out, just so I could never hear the sound again.

Whoa. Where did that bloodlust come from? I didn't remember ever wanting to harm someone the way this version of me did. She wanted to kill this woman in the most painful way possible, and she would like it.

The woman stopped laughing, clearing her throat and adjusting her floor-length, dark blue dress. It was a gown fit for a queen, but then again, she did have a crown. It only made sense. But what was she the queen of? Was she the one who put me in the tower?

"You don't understand, Eva." The woman grinned, her hands laced in front of her. "I've already gotten away with it. I've won, you lost. That's all there is to it. Now, you will spend the rest of eternity up in this tower. Never aging. Never dying." She stepped closer to me with each word, until she knelt before me. I jerked on my chains, my fingers reaching for her. "The only company you'll have is yourself, and after a few centuries, I'm sure even that will fade."

"You evil bitch," I spat at her, making her laugh once more.

"Isn't that the pot calling the kettle?" she asked, her hand coming up to cup my chin. "There is no punishment harsh enough for what you have done. For what you are. You are lucky the council would not allow me to kill you outright, or I'd have bathed in your blood as you bathed in my husband's." There was a sadness in her eyes, but the sharp righteousness to her tone almost made me overlook it.

I'd killed someone? The very thought chilled me to the bones. I couldn't imagine ever having drawn blood as this woman claimed. How had I forgotten so much in my time in the tower? Did my mind protect me from myself, or was there more?

"If I had to do it all again …" This version of myself began, her voice low and almost apologetic but I could feel it was false. My eyes flashed up with a wicked grin. "I would do it again, but make sure it lasted. Really draw out his screams." A haughty giggle escaped my lips, and the woman threw my face out of her hands, making my head bounce off the wall behind me.

"I don't see how my father could have ever loved you." The woman shook her head sadly. "What would he think if he saw you now?"

Her words seemed to sober me. The laughter died, and a frown twisted on my lips. "Your father was a fool who only loved me for my appearance. He could never see past your mother to see me for who I truly am."

"And now he never will." She lifted a shoulder and dropped it, shaking her head. "I hope you remember this. They assured me the spell wouldn't stop your mind, only your body. So, you will have your beauty, which you hold so dearly." Her eyes scanned over my form as she moved over to the window. The door I had escaped through no longer there. The spell must already be in place.

"Someone will find me," I told her, a last-ditch effort either to reassure myself or warn her. "You can't hide me away forever, and when they do...and they will...I will come for you first." I pulled on my chains until the metal bit into my wrists.

"What do I care?" The woman lifted a hand, dismissing my threat. "I'll be dead long before anyone ever finds you. So, hold on to your vengeance, because that's all you'll have *now. That and time." She smiled cruelly and climbed out of the window.*

I jerked and pulled at my bonds, desperation and outrage fueling my movements. "This isn't over, Snow. It will never be over," I screamed, fighting as hard as I could. "I will kill you and your children, and your children's children. Just you wait. I'll kill you all!"

I screamed until I awoke with a jerk, my throat raw and tears falling down my cheeks.

My eyes shot open, and I saw the stone walls surrounding me and the predicament I was in, and the fresh betrayal came rushing back. They were right to lock me up, though their reasoning behind it was not what it should be.

If they knew what I really was, the men who saved me would never have let me out of that tower. They might have very well killed me on the spot. The thought of Adam or even Luke looking at me with the same disgust and hatred that Snow did made my heart ache more than it already did.

They couldn't find out who I was. What I was. The woman in my dream was undeniably me. Or a version of me. And I didn't want that person anywhere near my mages, because she had made a promise, one that I had no doubt she would fight to fulfill if I let her.

A curse on the woman Snow and all her descendants. I didn't know who they were and really didn't care. I didn't have any intentions of finding them and carrying out that promise.

What I truly wanted to know was who had let me out? Who knew where I was hidden and allowed the monster that I was to be released back on the world? In my heart, I knew that I had not been good, not in any sense of the word. There was darkness and evil inside of me. Something that had morphed from hatred into some living, breathing need for vengeance, turning that version of me into a monster.

And she would have all the mages burn.

About the Author

Erin Bedford is an otaku, recovering coffee addict, and Legend of Zelda fanatic. Her brain is so full of stories that need to be told that she must get them out or explode into a million screaming chibis. Obsessed with fairy tales and bad boys, she hasn't found a story she can't twist to match her deviant mind full of innuendos, snarky humor, and dream guys.

On the outside, she's a work from home mom and bookbinger. One the inside, she's a thirteen-year-old boy screaming to get out and tell you the pervy joke they found online. As an ex-computer programmer, she dreams of one day combining her love for writing and college credits to make the ultimate video game!

Until then, when she's not writing, Erin is devouring as many books as possible on her quest to have the biggest book gut of all time. She's written over thirty books, ranging from paranormal romance, urban fantasy, and even scifi romance.

Come chat me up!
www.erinbedford.com
Facebook.com/erinrbedford
twitter.com/erin_bedford
Don't forget to follow me on Goodreads, Pinterest, Instagram, and YouTube!

Want to be the first to know about my new releases?
Erinbedford.com/newsletter

www.ingram.content.com/pod-product-compliance
Lightning Source LLC
Chambersburg PA
CBHW071754190726
48292CB00003B/980